With One Lousy Free Packet of Seed

Lynne Truss is a writer and broadcaster who started out as a literary editor with a blue pencil and then got sidetracked. The author of the bestselling *Eats, Shoots & Leaves*, she has written three other novels, *Going Loco*, *Making the Cat Laugh* and *Tennyson's Gift*, and numerous radio comedy dramas. Lynne Truss spent six years as the television critic of *The Times*, followed by four (rather peculiar) years as a sports columnist on the same newspaper. She won Columnist of the Year for her work for *Woman's Journal*. She now reviews books for the *Sunday Times* and is a familiar voice on BBC Radio 4. In 2002 she presented *Cutting a Dash*, a well-received Radio 4 series about punctuation ('a sparkling series of essays' – *Daily Telegraph*), which led to the writing of *Eats, Shoots & Leaves*.

ALSO BY LYNNE TRUSS

Eats, Shoots & Leaves

Going Loco
Making the Cat Laugh
Tennyson's Gift

With One Lousy Free Packet of Seed

LYNNE TRUSS

PROFILE BOOKS

Published in Great Britain in 2004 by Profile Books
PROFILE BOOKS LTD
58A Hatton Garden
London EC1N 8LX
www.profilebooks.co.uk

Previously published in 1994 by Penguin Books

3 5 7 9 10 8 6 4

Typeset in Quadraat by MacGuru Ltd
info@macguru.org.uk

Printed and bound in Great Britain by
Bookmarque Ltd, Croydon, Surrey

A CIP catalogue record for this book is available from the British Library.

ISBN 1 86197 749 2

I

Not having a hand free for a more dignified entrance, Osborne gave the swing door a mighty push with his foot, so that it boomed and echoed where it struck the wall beyond. 'Bugger,' he said, and shuffled awkwardly through the gap, sliding his back along the door to keep it open. He was distinctly overladen. From each wrist dangled various coloured string bags, bulging with parcels, fruit and scarves; and across his chest (as though to break an expected fall) he wore an old BOAC airline bag stuffed thick with dog-eared papers.

The subdued brown editorial offices of *Come Into the Garden*, though accustomed to having their peace-and-quiet vacuum broken by this weekly intrusion, gave a collective wince at Osborne's rough approach. The sudden draught of air that sucked the venetian blinds away from the windows and plucked the last rusting leaves from the parched, spindly weeping figs was like a sharp exasperated huff of disapproval. Someone once said you should never trust a doctor whose office plants had died. For some reason this dictum came back to haunt Osborne each week when he made his entrance. By the same token, you see, perhaps you should not pay too much attention to a weekly gardening magazine which looks as though it has just received a visit from Agent Orange.

'Ah,' he said (by way of greeting) to Lillian, the editor's secretary, but she made no reply. Her head thrown back at a tricky angle, Lillian was engrossed in savouring the last dregs of a cup-soup, tapping the vertical mug with a practised hand so that the last shards of soggy croûton came sliding and tumbling mouthwards, like rocks down a mountainside. Osborne knew from experience that there was no point expecting a response from Lillian while a single iota of monosodium glutamate remained at large. To judge from the distinctive aroma that hung like an iron curtain across the office, today's flavour was celery.

'Lillian?' A phone was ringing, and Osborne wondered vaguely whether someone should answer it.

'Lillian?'

'Ngh,' said Lillian, preoccupied with running her tongue around the inside of the mug.

'Shall I answer this?'

'Ngh, ngh,' replied Lillian.

'Right you are, then,' said Osborne cheerfully, and left it to ring.

Heaping his string bags on a free desk, he felt strangely happy. *Come Into the Garden* had always felt a bit like home to Osborne, a shelter where he was welcome and beloved. As a regular contributor, blown in weekly from the cold, he felt tended, nurtured – like a special potted geranium brought indoors by a caring husbandman at the first sharp sting of autumn frost. What colour geranium? you might ask, if you were a gardening person. Well, Osborne was not dogmatic on the subject, but in his mind's eye he leaned towards cerise. But the colour was largely immaterial. The point was that though he might be hibernating (professionally speaking) at *Come Into the Garden*, at least he was not in imminent danger of rusting, wilting, perishing, or being hoicked out and shredded for compost. And occasionally

– to push the geranium analogy to its furthest limit – a colleague with a kind heart and advanced ideas might even take the trouble to stop beside his desk and encourage him with a few kind words.

So every Wednesday Osborne came to the office to compose his time-honoured 'Me and My Shed' column and soak up the atmosphere. These pieces could equally well be written at home, really (in fact, the idea had been suggested to him more than once), but throughout his career he had always written in offices, from his early days as a staff reporter on a South Coast evening paper, and all through his time as a second-string drama critic in the sixties, so it was how he felt most comfortable. Physically, being a large, broad-shouldered person, he looked slightly out of place at an office desk, as if when he stood up he would tip it over. But Osborne merely felt cosy. He warmed to the very mottoes on the walls – 'Ne'er cast a clout till May be out'; 'It is not spring until you can plant your foot upon twelve daisies' – and thought of the parable of the seed on fertile ground. Also, not for the first time, he wondered whether anyone on the staff actually had a garden.

A man who has been buffeted by life needs a place where he can lay down his string bags. He needs a place where he can sit at an old Tipp-Ex-spattered Adler, treat himself to a free cup of tea, miss his deadline by hours, stand helpless at the photocopier until someone rescues him, fill his pockets at the stationery cupboard, and make hour-long surreptitious phone calls to old journo muckers in faraway foreign parts. *Come Into the Garden* was that place for Osborne.

Today, however, it seemed there was no one about. Osborne removed a few thick, dank layers of navy-blue outdoor garment (the month was November) and hung them on a coat stand, which promptly collapsed under the weight. 'Bugger,' he said, and ran his fingers through his short, grey hair. Where was everybody? He looked around for clues. A half-empty mail-sack lay limp in the middle of Reception, but he was aware that little could be deduced from this. Lillian (who had now disappeared) famously claimed to have a medical problem with sorting the post, due to a rare neurotic-compulsive fear of envelopes. Such a condition was obviously unfortunate in a secretary (almost a disqualification, you might think), but there you were.

This unfortunate and improbable malady meant that post sorting was an all-day process, with a half-empty mail-sack permanently dumped on the floor as a kind of endless reproach, and most of the editorial staff sensibly steering well clear and simply learning never to depend too heavily on the prompt dispersal of correspondence. Lillian's wont was to stoop and sigh over a heap of letters, laboriously examining each one with the aid of tongs, and stopping chance passers-by with *faux-naif* questions evidently calculated to drive them mad. 'Look, this says "John Mainwaring, Editor",' she might say, waving the ironware in a wild, threatening manner, 'but the editor's name is *James* Mainwaring.' Here she would pause to ascertain what reaction she was getting (usually uneasy silence). 'What do you think? Shall I send it back, or pitch it in the bin?' No one ever knew what to say to this sort of thing; after all, you don't argue with mad people, especially when they are equipped to clock you with a pair of tongs. So Lillian got away with it, as she got away with everything else. And in between these bouts of petty tyranny, she would sit quietly at her desk, ignoring the phones, and give her full attention to the smoking of a cigarette – on the grounds, presumably, that if a thing is worth doing, it is worth doing well.

It seemed odd to be in the office on his own. Osborne was assailed by an understandable fear that he had forgotten an important appointment elsewhere – an appointment that his green-ink-fingered friends had evidently all remembered. Even the tireless sub-editors were missing from their work stations, and Osborne marvelled when he peered into their little book-lined room and saw their four empty chairs – a sight, he realized, that few people other than night cleaners had ever previously witnessed. The fabric on one of the chairs turned out to be a jaunty rich tartan – but no wonder he had never suspected it, when a sub-editor's drab, grey jumper and unkempt shirt (not to mention his drab, grey, unkempt body) had always blocked the view.

Like many writers, Osborne was afraid of sub-editors, the trouble being that they had a disarming habit of changing his prose automatically, without telling him. 'Ah, the further musings of the giant intellect,' the chief sub-editor might say, with gratuitous cruelty, as she took his copy each week; and then, the moment he had left the room, she fell on it savagely with a thick blue pen, taking out all the bits he was most proud of. In his more gloomy moments, he wondered why he bothered to write the piece in the first place, when the subsequent contribution of the sub-editor so often outweighed his own. He had been known to quote the lament of Macduff ('What, all my little chicks?') at the thought of his innocents, massacred. And you couldn't blame him. 'Not in my back yard' he had once confidently typed in a piece about a politician, only to discover, a few days later, in the printed magazine, that it had been rewritten as 'Not on my patio', which was not quite the same.

In the stealthy, unnatural quiet of the sub-editors' room, dictionaries and half-corrected proofs lay open on abandoned desks. Osborne tiptoed guiltily, like a schoolboy finding himself alone in an after-hours classroom when everyone has gone home. To stay his nerves, he helped himself to an Extra Strong Mint from a roll next to the chief sub-editor's typewriter (careful not to disarrange her impressive selection of nail varnishes), and peered from an awkward position at the proof she had been correcting, which was covered in tiny blue marks and explanatory notes circled with a feminine flourish. 'NOTE TO TYPESETTER,' he read, upside-down,

> Far be it from me etcetera, but it seems to me that despite our best efforts a *twinge* of confusion remains in your mind between 'forbear' – a verb meaning 'abstain or refrain from' – and 'forebear' – a noun denoting an ancestor. May we bid adieu to these intrusive 'e's? I hope this clears things up. I have mentioned this before, of course; but how can you be expected to remember? You lead such busy lives, and Radio 1 must absorb a lot of your attention. I do understand. Sorry to take up your valuable time. And far be it from me, etcetera.
>
> Michelle

Osborne gulped in amazement at such erudition, which was an unfortunate thing to do. For the Extra Strong Mint promptly closed over his windpipe, like a manhole cover over an orifice in the road.

Thus it was that when the three subs re-entered the room in wordless single file a few moments later, they discovered their 'Me and My Shed' columnist bent double with a gun-metal litter-bin held to his face, making mysterious amplified strangling noises. Since nothing louder than the whisper of a nail file was usually to be heard in this room, they naturally flashed their specs in annoyance. However, having all received the statutory sub-editor's training (involving, one suspects, the same kind of rigorous football-rattle personality testing undergone by the horses of riot police), they simply resumed their solemn work of skewering other people's chicks with their thick blue pens.

'Are you in difficulties, *mon cher?*' asked Michelle, the chief sub-editor, archly, adjusting an embroidered collar and seating herself carefully so as not to rumple her dirndl skirt. Osborne shook his head (and litter-bin) emphatically, to indicate that any difficulties were of only passing significance. The sub-editors swapped glances (or did they signal Morse code with those specs?) and sighed. Osborne discharged the mint with a loud *ptang-yang* sound and fled red-faced from the room, and all was peace again.

It was quite some time before Osborne discovered the reason for the empty office; obviously, if he had asked a few questions, there and then, he might have been saved a lot of the palaver of the ensuing week. Unfortunately, however, he did not. The fact was, there had been a crisis meeting. The magazine had been sold to a new proprietor; a new editor had been mentioned, along with a rationalization of the staff. He did not yet know it, but a cold wind was blowing at *Come Into the Garden*; his shelter had been torn up and blown away, like so much matchwood.

However, since nobody had yet informed him of this, Osborne merely dragged his airline bag to his favourite corner, and from a safe distance waved hello again to Lillian. She was flicking through a mail order catalogue now, turning each page with a practised insouciant finger-technique not involving the thumb, while a motorbike messenger stood in front of her desk, waiting for her to look up. Above her head, Osborne noticed, there was a new sign. It said, 'What did your last slave die of?'

He produced his notebook, flipped a few pages and attempted to compose his thoughts. Now, Osborne, old buddy, who have you got for us this week? He typed the words ME AND MY SHED at the top of a sheet of paper, and added a colon.

ME AND MY SHED:

A name ought to follow, but for some reason it failed to come. Osborne frowned. Every week he interviewed a famous person about their shed – *Me and My Shed: Melvyn Bragg; Me and My Shed: Stirling Moss.* He had been doing it for years. In certain professional quarters people still raved about his *Me and My Shed: David Essex*; it was said that for anyone interested in the art of celebrity outhouse interviewing, it had represented the absolute 'last word'. Osborne treasured this praise, while in general being modest about his job, deflecting the envy of non-journalists by saying merely that he had seen the insides of some classy sheds in his time. But today, despite remembering a bus journey to Highgate on Monday morning – despite, moreover, remembering the interior fittings of the shed in some considerable detail – it was only the classiness of the shed that stuck in his mind. He just could not put a classy face to it. The words

ME AND MY SHED:

looked up accusingly from the typewriter. Especially the colon on the end.

He flicked through his notes again, but they offered little help. After twelve years of writing 'Me and My Shed' he had come to the unsurprising conclusion that all sheds are alike in the dark. Even when the column's remit had been extended, in the mid-1980s, to include greenhouses and any other temporary garden structures (such as the ivy-covered car-port), the interviews had always required a masterly touch to bring them alive. Here, for example, was a sample of this week's notes:

> Had shed since bght house. Quite good sh. Spend time in sh. obv. Also gd 4 keeping thngs in. Never done anythng to sh, particrly. Cat got locked in sh once, qu funny. Don't thnk abt sh often. Take sh for grantd. Sorry. Not v interstng. *House* interestng. Sh not.

Time was pressing, The official deadline was 2.30, and it was now a quarter past twelve. Osborne typed a few words, hoping that the act of writing might jog his memory. He looked out of the window and tried to free-associate about Highgate, but curiously found himself thinking about Marmite sandwiches on a windswept beach, so gave it up. The experience of thirty years in journalism, a dozen of them in sheds, seemed to have deserted him.

In fact, he was just beginning to consider turning the column into a kind of mystery slot this week, calling it 'Who and Whose Shed?', when Tim, the deputy editor, ambled past, carrying a page proof towards the subs' room. Tim was one of those aforementioned people who sometimes dropped a few encouraging words in the direction of a torpid geranium, and he did so now. But it was no big deal, actually. Tim was a thin, aloof young fellow (twenty-four, twenty-five?) with a generally abstracted air, tight pullovers and bottle-thick kick-me specs; a young man whose emotional thermostat had been set too low at an early age, and was now too stiff to budge. Now he stopped at Osborne's side and crouched down to read on the typewriter 'Me and My Shed's' recently composed opening sentence:

> When the cat got stuck in the shed for 24 hours last year, there were red faces all round at a certain house in Highgate.

Tim wrinkled his nose and chewed his biro. 'So?' he asked. 'How did things go with Angela Farmer?'

Osborne thought for a second. Angela Farmer?

'Quite a coup getting her, I thought,' continued Tim. 'In fact, I made a note somewhere. I think we'll splash it. Nice to have your name on the front of the magazine again before –'

Tim stopped abruptly, but Osborne didn't notice. He was experiencing a strange sense of weightlessness. Was it possible to meet Angela Farmer, glamorous middle-aged American star of a thousand British sitcoms, and have no recollection of it? He tried picturing the scene at the door, the handshake, the famous smoky voice of Ms Farmer barking, 'C'min! What're ya waitin for? Applause?' but nothing came. His mind was a blank; *it was as though he had never met her*. Panic welled in his chest, and in a split second his entire career as a celebrity interviewer flashed before his eyes.

'So what was she like?'

'Is it hot in here?'

'Yes, a bit. But what was she like?'

Osborne decided to bluff.

'Angela Farmer? Oh, fine. Fine, Angela Farmer, yes. Very' – here he consulted his notes – 'interesting. Very American, of course.'

Tim nodded encouragingly.

'Good shed, was it?'

'Angela Farmer's shed, you mean? Yes, oh yes. Ms Farmer has a surprisingly good shed.'

'Did you ask about those hilarious gerbils in the shed in *From This Day Forward*?'

'Did I? Oh yes, I'm sure I did.'

'And I think I read somewhere that she was actually proposed to in a shed by her second husband – whatsisname, the man who plays the shed builder in *For Ever and Ever Amen* – but that they broke up after a row about weather-proofing.'

'All true, mate. All true.'

'Should make an interesting piece, then.'

'I'll say.'

They both paused, staring into the middle distance, pondering the interesting piece. 'The cat got stuck in the shed overnight once, too.'

'What's that?'

'The cat. Got stuck in the shed. Overnight. She said it was quite funny.'

The deputy editor wrinkled his nose again, and changed the subject.

'Oh, and you ought to mention the Angela Farmer rose. Smash hit of last year's Chelsea. No doubt propagated in a shed, of course, ha ha. But I expect you covered all that.'

Osborne gave a brave smile.

'Well, mustn't hold you up.'

'No.'

'See you later.'

'Yes.'

'Don't you ever get tired of sheds, Osborne?'

'Never.'

'Unlike some,' said the deputy editor darkly, and girded himself to do battle with the subs.

Waiting for Osborne's column later that evening, after everyone else had gone home, Michelle donned her pastry-cuffs, strapped a spotless pinny over her outfit, and tackled the reference books, rearranging them in strict alphabetical order, fixing them in a perpendicular position, and drawing them neatly to the extreme edge of the shelves. Having accomplished this, she scoured the coffee machine and dusted the venetian blinds, in the course of which activity she deliberately elbowed a large economy packet of Lillian's cup-soups into a bin. Then she sat down at her typewriter and wrote some much-needed letters for the 'Dear Donald' page.

She loved this task. Few bona fide readers were writing to the magazine these days, and Michelle's particular joy was to write the bogus letters ungrammatically and then correct them afterwards. Subbing was a great passion of Michelle's; it was like making a plant grow straight and tall. 'Dear Donald,' she would type with a thrill. 'As an old age pensioner, my Buddleia has grown too big for me to comfortably cut it back myself ...' She could barely prevent herself from ripping it straight out of the machine, to prune those dangling modifiers, stake those split infinitives. How quickly the time passed when you were having fun. The only thing that stumped her – as it always did – was the invention of fake names and addresses, because she could never see why one fake name sounded more authentic than any other. 'G. Clarke, Honiton, Devon' was how she signed each one of today's batch, hoping that inspiration would strike later. She often chose G. Clarke of Honiton. She'd never been there, but she fancied that's where all the readers lived.

Time to check up on Osborne, she thought, when ten letters from G. Clarke were complete, photocopied and subbed within an inch of their lives. She dialled Osborne's number on the internal phone. It rang on his desk and startled him, so that he dropped an open bottle of Tipp-Ex on to his shoes.

'Bugger,' he said, as he answered the phone.

'Going well, oh great wordsmith?'

Kneading his face, Osborne watched in helpless alarm as the correcting fluid seeped into the leather uppers of his only decent footwear.

'Anything wrong?'

'No, no. Nearly there, actually. Just got to think of the pay-off.'

'Oh marvellous.' Michelle sounded ironic, the way she often did on Wednesday nights. 'That's dandy.'

There was a pause.

'Far be it from me,' she said sweetly, 'but have you mentioned that he writes in his shed? And that this explains the repeated use of weed-killer as a murder weapon in the books? You know what I mean: he looks up from his rude desk of logs for inspiration, and there's the weed-killer, next to the bone-meal. In the one I took on holiday last year, he killed off the prime suspect with a garden rake. One blow to the back of the neck, and that was it. Nasty. In the latest book, I understand, someone is dealt the death-blow with a pair of shears.'

'What are you talking about? Who do you mean?'

'Trent Carmichael. This week's "Me and My Shed". The crime writer.'

Osborne thought a minute, thought another minute, remembered everything – in particular the bestselling author laughing apologetically, 'Well, er, the cat got locked in the shed once, but no foul play was suspected!' – and said, 'I'll call you back.'

Things were looking bad. He unlaced his shoes, took them off, and on bended knee started to scrub them upside down on the carpet, hoping to remove the worst of the whitener while deciding what to do next. He looked up to see Michelle standing beside him.

'No, you've got it wrong,' he said, keeping his eyes on the floor, his pulse pounding in his neck. 'Trent Carmichael is next week. You wouldn't know whether this stuff washes out, would you?'

'So who is it this week?'

'Angela Farmer,' he mumbled.

'Who?'

'Angela Farmer.'

'No. Are you sure?'

'Of course I'm sure.'

'That's very odd.'

'No, I met her on Monday. Not odd at all. Nice woman.'

Michelle narrowed her eyes as though to contest the point, and then decided not to bother. She stretched her arms instead; this conversation clearly had nowhere to go.

'How nice,' she said. 'I'd better not hold you up, then. Have you mentioned she's got a tulip named after her?'

'I thought it was a rose.'

'No, tulip.'

Osborne looked like he might be sick.

'Tell you what,' said Michelle. 'It's been a hard day, I'll look it up for you.'

Osborne sat in his stockinged feet, stroking the keys of his typewriter and staring into space. In all his years as a journalist, he had never before written up an interview that had not taken place. Why ever had he believed Tim? Tim didn't *know*. How, moreover, could he extricate himself now he had gone so far? Not only had he cast all Trent Carmichael's faint and unamusing witticisms into a broad American slang, but he was now also stuck with sentences referring to (a) love being like a red red tulip, and (b) a woman who viewed the world through tulip-tinted spectacles.

In fact, he was so absorbed in his confusion and dismay that he did not hear the phone ringing, nor hear Michelle answer it. What he did hear, however (and quite distinctly), was Michelle informing him that it had been Angela Farmer phoning to apologize. She would have to postpone their appointment for the following Monday, making it Tuesday instead. She suggested that since she lived in the West Country, he might like to use Monday as a travelling day and stay overnight at a local hotel, details of which she had passed on to Michelle.

'She sounded very nice,' said Michelle, studying Osborne's pole-axed expression.

'That's lovely,' said Osborne.

'Oh, and she hoped it wasn't too inconvenient – to ring so late in the day.'

2

Osborne dunked a piece of peanut brittle in his coffee and reflected. Perhaps it was time to bail out of this shed business before serious damage was done. From his favourite breakfast corner in his local Cypriot dossers' café on a bleak November Friday (his belongings tucked around him like sandbags against a blast) he looked mournfully at the bright, mass-produced pictures of mythical Greek heroes adorning the walls and asked himself whether the cutting edge of outhouse journalism had not finally proved too much for him. A vision of Michelle sending him home two nights ago on a tide of unreassuring platitudes ('It could happen to anyone, Osborne; but funny how it happened to you'), and then expertly recasting his article with firm unanswerable blue strokes (and well-informed references to Trent Carmichael's favourite horticultural murder weapons), rose unbidden to his mind and gave him torment. He stared at a picture of Perseus amid the gorgons and emitted a low moan.

'Me and My Shed' had had its sticky moments in the past, but nothing ever like this. In the course of a dozen years' trouble-shooting around celebrity gardens Osborne had been exposed to a variety of dangers – hostile rabbits, wobbly paving and possibly harmful levels of creosote – but none had shaken his confidence to a comparable degree. Not even when he was mistaken for the man from *The Times* and treated to a lengthy reminiscence of a painful Somerset childhood (none of it involving sheds, incidentally, or outbuildings of any kind) had he felt so pig-sick about himself, despite the extreme embarrassment all round when that particular ghastly mistake was finally uncovered. (It had been a terrifying example of cross purposes at work, incidentally, since for a considerable time the interviewee supposed that Osborne's repeated prompting 'And did *that* happen in a shed?' was evidence of a deep-seated emotional disturbance almost on a par with his own.)

Osborne did not particularly relish recalling his past humiliations, but while he was on the subject he was compelled to admit there had been few things worse than the time he was locked in a shed by a hyperactive child, who then cunningly reported to its celebrity father that 'the man in the smelly coat' had been called away on urgent business. Luckily, an old woman had let him out, but only after four hours had passed. Interestingly, this was the incident Osborne generally called to mind when he overheard people say, 'We'll probably laugh about all this later on' – because he had learned that there were certain miseries in life which Time signally failed to transform into anything even slightly resembling a rib-tickler, and spending four unplanned hours hammering on the inside of a Lumberland Alpine Resteezy was definitely among them.

'All right, mate?'

A man in a tight, battered baseball cap touched Osborne by the sleeve, and he jerked out of his reverie – which was just as well, because it was turning grim.

'What's that?'

'All right, are you, mate? Your coffee's got cold.'

'Thanks. Right. Oh bugger, yes,' said Osborne, and stirred his coffee very quickly, as though the frantic action might jiggle the molecules sufficiently to reheat it.

In front of him on the table lay his morning's post, still unopened, and he looked at it with his eyes deliberately half-closed, so that it looked sort of blurry and distant, and a bit less threatening. None of the envelopes resembled his monthly cheque; most, he knew only too well, would be scratchy xeroxed brochures for self-assembly Lumberland Alpines. He recognized immediately the familiar postmark betokening a personal reader's letter 'sent on' from the magazine, and put it automatically to one side. True, sometimes a reader's letter could cheer him up enormously ('Another marvellous insight into a famous life!' somebody wrote once, in handwriting very similar to his sister's), but quite often Osborne's correspondents were OAP gardening fanatics who not only entertained very fixed ideas about the virtues of terracotta (as opposed to plastic), but allowed these ideas full dismal rein in wobbly joined-up handwriting on lined blue Basildon Bond.

Where was Makepeace? They had agreed to meet at 11.30, and it was after twelve. Why was Makepeace always late for these meetings? It is a general rule, of course, that the person with the least distance to travel will contrive to show up last. But Makepeace lived upstairs from the café, for goodness' sake. This was why they had chosen the Birthplace of Aphrodite as their particular weekly rendezvous. He was up there now, in all probability, while Osborne had the job of retaining his claim to the table by the age-old custom of not finishing his food and saying, 'Excuse me, whoops, I'm sorry –' every time a table-clearer wielding a damp grey cloth attempted to remove his plate. In fact, he had spent much of the past fifteen minutes holding the plate down quite firmly with both hands, as though trying to bond it to the formica by sheer effort of push.

'So,' said Makepeace, sitting down opposite. 'Where have *you* been?' He appeared out of nowhere: just materialized on the seat as though he had suddenly grown there, *whoosh*, like a time-lapse sunflower in a nature programme. He was always doing this, Makepeace; creeping up on people. It was terribly unsettling. Once, he crept up on Osborne outside an off-licence, with the result that the six bottles of Beck's that Osborne had just invited home for a little party suddenly found they had an alternative urgent appointment getting smashed to bits on the pavement. Now, at the Birthplace of Aphrodite, the effect was less catastrophic (it did not require a dustpan and brush), but Osborne was nevertheless startled sufficiently to let go of the plate, which was whisked away instantly by a triumphant cloth-lady.

Osborne sometimes speculated how the world must appear to someone like Makepeace – given the effect he had on it himself. You know the old theory that the royal family think the world smells of fresh paint, that the Queen assumes people talk endlessly on brief acquaintance about the minutiae of their jobs and the distance they've travelled to be present? Well, similarly Makepeace, with his unfortunate, disarming habit of misplaced stealth, must surely assume that the world was full of people who greet you by leaping in the air and shouting 'Gah!' in alarm. He must also, by extension, know a proportionately large number of people who worry ostentatiously about the current state of their tickers.

'Gah!' shouted Osborne. 'Makepeace! Hey! Bugger me! Phew!'

'Well, of course; bugger me, exactly,' repeated Makepeace slowly, without much enthusiasm, as he gently peeled off his denim jacket, folded it as though it were linen or silk, and adjusted his long, ginger pony-tail so that it hung neatly down his back. 'But what the hell kept you, my friend?'

Osborne looked quizzically into Makepeace's blank blue eyes and considered what to say.

'What do you mean? I –'

'We agreed 11.30, didn't we? Well, I put my head round the

door ten minutes ago – ten to bloody twelve – and *you* weren't here. I was beginning to think that *you* weren't coming.'

'Listen, I don't get this,' protested Osborne. 'I was here all the time.'

Makepeace pursed his lips in disbelief.

'Didn't see you, pal.'

'Well, I was.'

Makepeace put up his palms as if to say, 'Don't be so defensive,' and then changed his tone.

'Listen, you're here now and that's what matters.'

'Hang on, you can ask any –'

But Osborne faltered and gave up. In the circumstances, actually, this was the only sensible course of action. Having known Makepeace only a couple of months, he had already learned one very useful thing – that you could never, ever place him in the wrong. Osborne had met know-alls in the past; he had been acquainted with big-heads, too. But Makepeace was both know-all and big-head, with an added complication. Conceivably, he was a psychopath.

'Son,' his daddy must have said to him at an impressionable age, 'never apologize, never explain. Is that clear? Also, deny absolutely everything that doesn't suit you, even in the teeth of outright contrary proof. Now, all right, let's have it, what did I just tell you?'

'Tell me?' Makepeace must have hotly replied. 'You told me nothing! What the hell are you talking about? I just came through the door, and you're asking me a load of stupid questions.'

At which his daddy presumably chuckled (in a sinister fond-father-of-the-growing-psychopath sort of way) and said, 'That's my boy.'

Makepeace was younger than Osborne, thirty-five to Osborne's forty-eight, but sometimes seemed to aspire to an emotional age of six. Wiry and five foot two, and usually attired in blue denim, he had a long face and a short, flat nose, so that Osborne was involuntarily reminded of a stunted, mean-looking infant pressing his face hard against a cake-shop window. It was easy to feel sorry for the little chap: parents warning their children against the dangers of smoking or masturbation had been known to point to him – unfortunately, in his hearing – as an example of the worst that could happen. Makepeace rose above all this by being clever, of course; and with a couple of good university degrees behind him, he presently made a fairly decent, grown-up living from writing erudite book reviews for national newspapers and periodicals, in which he used his great capacities as a professional know-all as a perfectly acceptable substitute for either insight or style.

There was, however, still a tears-before-bedtime quality to Makepeace's existence, which compelled Osborne to worry on his behalf. The trouble was that this prodigy, precisely in the manner of a precocious child, was utterly unable to judge the point at which he had delighted the grown-ups beyond endurance. Thus, having acquired a reputation for his readiness to write a thousand words on any subject under heaven (*he* would have written the Angela Farmer thing without a qualm, even knowing that it was all a fraud), he now faced a quite serious problem, in that his extraordinary level of output was beginning to outstrip plausibility. People had started to notice that he wrote more book reviews in a week than was technically possible, yet if you suggested he hadn't read the books with any degree of diligence, he would instantly offer to knock you down.

His various editors guessed that he might not be reading very carefully, but it was difficult to prove; and Makepeace was indeed an extraordinarily compelling liar, with a particular flair for outright incandescent denial. On the regular occasions when he missed a deadline (through sheer bottleneck of work) he would never admit it, but instead swore hotly that he had personally fed each sheet of his review into a fax machine – and without missing a beat he would go on to explain in a regretful tone that he would dearly love to send it again, had it not been: (a) snatched from his hands by a freak typhoon in Clapham High Street; (b) burgled from his flat; or (c) lent to a friend who had just boarded a flight to Venezuela. 'Tell you what, though, I can type it out again by Friday,' he would offer, fooling nobody. And somehow he always got away with it.

The curious thing, of course, was that while Osborne knew all this, he liked him anyway. Makepeace made him laugh. Also, Osborne enjoyed in his company the novel sensation of feeling relatively grown up. So he introduced Makepeace to more editors, and even arranged for him to review gardening books for Tim on the magazine. His one ridiculous error was in thinking he ought to explain a few basic gardening terms that Makepeace might not be familiar with. On this gross, unforgivable insult, their relationship nearly foundered. You just could not tell Makepeace something he didn't already know; it was as simple as that. Sitting in this very Birthplace of Aphrodite one afternoon, and regarding the Greek pictures on the walls, Osborne had learned this lesson the hard way when a civilized difference of opinion about aetiological myths had hurtled seriously out of control.

They had been talking – as all literary people will, from time to time – of the legend of Persephone, whom Hades famously stole from the earth to make Nature mourn (thus proving the existence of winter, or something). Anyway, the question was this: had Persephone eaten six pomegranates while underground, or six pomegranate *seeds?* Osborne said seeds, and afterwards checked it in a book at the library. And he was right. Naïvely assuming that only the truth was at issue, he made a mental note to pass on the information to his friend when next they met. After all, seeds were probably significant, seeing as the myth was concerned with seasonal renewal, and all that.

So next time he saw Makepeace he mentioned their discussion and said, quite innocently, that yes, it was seeds.

There was a fractional pause, and then Makepeace said, 'Yes, seeds. That's what I said.'

Osborne gasped at the lie, and then giggled.

'No, you didn't.'

'Yes, I did.'

Makepeace wasn't joking. He should have been, but he wasn't.

'No. You didn't. You said she ate pomegranates, that's different. It was me who said it was seeds.'

'You're wrong.'

'Look, I'm sorry, but this is really silly, and it's not worth arguing about, but you really did say pomegranates. You *argued* with me, don't you remember?'

'I fucking *didn't*.'

'Makepeace, what's the big deal here? I don't understand. Why can't you admit you were wrong?'

At which point Makepeace stood up so abruptly that his chair fell over backwards, and bellowed, '*What the fucking hell are you talking about?*'

It had been a tricky moment.

'What's all the stuff?' asked Makepeace now, reading Osborne's envelopes upside-down.

'My post. I can't face it.'

'Do you want me to open it?'

'No.'

'Oh, come on,' said Makepeace, and picked up the envelope with the *Come Into the Garden* postmark.

'Not that one,' protested Osborne, but it was too late. Makepeace had already taken out two sheets of paper and started to read them.

'Odd,' he said, shuffling the pages one behind the other, and frowning. 'This is dead odd.' He read them both a couple of times, and then handed them to Osborne.

> Dear Mr Lonsdale [said the first],
> I have long been a fan of your column. Being a keen gardener myself, your insights into sheds of the famous fill me with interest. I think you are probably a nice man. I can imagine you wearing a nice coat and scarf and slippers possibly. Also smoking a pipe, quite distinguished. While I am wearing not much while writing this actually. Just a thin négligé and some gold flip-flops. And green-thumb gardening gloves.
>
> Phew, it's hot work, gardening. I am not a celebrity like Melvyn Bragg and Anna Ford but I would let you rummage in my shed if you asked me!! I've got all sorts of odds and ends that nobody knows about tucked away behind the flower-pots. If you catch my drift.
>
> Yours affectionately,
> G. Clarke,
> Honiton, Devon

Osborne was slightly embarrassed. But at least it made a change from the terracotta maniacs. He finished his coffee in a single swig, and shrugged at Makepeace.

'Mad, I expect,' he said.

'There's more,' said Makepeace.

Osborne shuffled the papers and found the second letter, identically typed, and on the same-sized paper as the first. It seemed to be from the same person, but it had a distinctly different tone.

> Dear Mr Lonsdale,
> Having counted no less than 15 errors of fact (not to mention grammar) in your last 'Me and My Shed' column, isn't it time you stopped pretending to be a journalist? Call yourself a writer well I don't think. I could do better myself, and thats saying something.

I haven't even *met* Trent Carmichael. How much longer must we be subjected to this slapdash twaddle masquerading as journalism? I am surprised anyone agrees to be interviewed by you. Do you know *you make all the sheds sound the same?* Why does a magazine of such evident quality continue to employ you? Stay out of sheds and do us a favour.

G. Clarke,
Honiton, Devon

P.S. Someone ought to lock you in a shed and throw away the key.

'What do you think?' asked Makepeace.
'Bugger,' said Osborne.

Lillian lit a cigarette, narrowing her eyes against the smoke, and looked round to check that no one was watching. Coughing, she leaned back and continued to ignore the ringing of the phone. There is a cool, insolent way that blonde, permanent-waved secretaries inspect their fingernails in old *film noir* movies, and Lillian, a baby blonde herself in an electric-blue angora woolly, attempted it now, arching her eyebrows like Marlene Dietrich; but then suddenly broke the illusion by tearing off the broken top of her thumbnail with a savage rip from her teeth. She looked round again, smiling, spat the nail expertly into a waste-paper basket and tried momentarily to imagine what it would be like to be deaf.

Since the announcement of the takeover of *Come Into the Garden*, the phone had not stopped ringing. The newspapers were not very interested; but readers would phone in panic, selfishly demanding reassurance that the magazine would not cease publication just when the greenfly problem was at its height, or when the monthly 'Build your own greenhouse' series reached a crucial stage in the glazing. Lillian fielded these inquiries in a variety of ways. For example, sometimes she simply unplugged the phone. At other times she answered, but pretended to be speaking from the swimming baths. And sometimes, as now, she sat and suffered its ringing, perched on her typist's chair with her legs crossed and with her eyes fixed steadily on the ceiling.

To add to the picture of martyrdom, a new sign hung above her desk, with the legend 'Is Peace and Quiet So Much to Ask?' But a keen-eyed observer might also notice that today Lillian was mixing her metaphors, for her corner of the office was adorned with items suggestive less of pietism than of couch potato. A fluffy rug had appeared; also a standard lamp, a magazine rack and a basket with knitting in it. Half a sitting-room, in fact, had blossomed overnight where previously had stood only furniture and fittings appropriate to the office of a small magazine. She was not using this stuff yet, but it was there, and it was obviously permanent. It was a statement of intent.

Apart from the phone ringing, the office was quiet again. Friday was the day when most of the editorial staff decamped to the typesetters, to sit on broken chairs in a makeshift work-room from six in the morning and wait miserably all day for proofs to correct. Lillian had never visited the typesetters, and imagined it, rather perversely, as some sort of holiday camp. The word 'buns' had once been mentioned in her hearing, and this had unaccountably conjured to her mind a scene of great frivolity, like something Christmassy in Dickens. Perhaps she thought the sub-editors tossed these buns across the room at each other, or had races to pick out the most currants or lemon peel. Who knows? Envy can play funny tricks on a person's mind. Anyway, the fact that Tim and Michelle would return late on Friday afternoons actually stumbling with fatigue failed utterly to shake Lillian's notion of Typesetter Heaven. 'No, I'm afraid Michelle is not in the office today,' she would report to the editor (who sometimes popped in on Fridays to check his post for job offers). 'She has got the day off, at the typesetters. I expect she will be back at work next week.'

Suddenly, on a whim, Lillian answered the phone.

'Come Into the Garden,' she snapped, making sure it didn't sound too much like an invitation.

'For heaven's sake, Lillian, where were you?'

It was Michelle. Lillian pursed her lips and made a series of smoke rings by jabbing her cigarette in the air.

'Did you say where was I?' she repeated carefully. 'Well, I'll tell you. I was stuck in the bloody lift, that's where I was.'

Michelle ignored this. Life was too short to argue about it.

'Listen, could I be a desperate bore and ask you to do something for me? I brought my "Dear Donald" file with me, and a couple of letters are missing. Would you be unbelievably selfless and helpful, and look on my desk for them?'

Lillian prepared to stand up, but then thought better of it.

'The letters to Osborne from Honiton?'

'What?' Michelle sounded rather indistinct, suddenly.

'The letters to Osborne. From Honiton.'

'No,' she said, after a noticeable pause. 'Ha ha, I don't think I've seen any letters to Osborne. No. Not from Honiton, I don't think. Hmm. I mean, surely they would be sent straight to him, wouldn't they? Nothing to do with "Dear Donald". Or to do with *me*, for that matter.'

'I suppose not.'

Lillian waited. She had known Michelle for fifteen years. This pally 'ha ha' business told her something was up. The seconds ticked by. 'So,' said Michelle at last, 'have you *got* the letters to Osborne? I wouldn't mind a peek.'

'No can do, I'm afraid. I sent them on yesterday.'

Michelle gasped.

'To Osborne?'

'That's right.'

'Oh.'

'Nothing wrong, I hope?'

'No, it's fine.'

Lillian took a deep, satisfying drag on the cigarette. 'By the way, you haven't seen my big packet of cup-soups by any chance?'

Osborne turned the letters over in his hands, and felt peculiar. Peculiar was the only word for it. Makepeace meanwhile took a large bite out of a fried-egg sandwich and tried to imagine what it would be like to realize one morning that you had a fan in the West Country who entertained schizophrenic delusions about you while dressed in gold flip-flops and reinforced gloves. It was hard.

'I don't like this bit about slapdash twaddle,' said Osborne at last.

'Hmm,' agreed Makepeace.

'I mean, what does she take me for? You don't expect Tolstoy in a piece about sheds, surely?'

Makepeace grunted, wiped some egg-yolk from his chin and prepared to contest the point. 'Except that all happy sheds are happy in the same way, I suppose,' he volunteered, reaching for a serviette. 'While unhappy sheds . . .' But he tailed off, sensing he had lost his audience. Osborne looked nonplussed.

'I suppose we are sure it's a woman,' added Makepeace. 'I mean, the négligé might be more interesting than it at first appears.'

Osborne looked mournfully at the infant Hercules wrestling with snakes (next to the tea-urn) and shook his head.

'So who's the next shed, then?'

'Ah,' said Osborne darkly, as though it meant something. 'Angela Farmer.'

'Where's the problem? Right up your street. Funny, charming, famous. Didn't she have a rose named after her recently?'

'It was a tulip.'

'That's right. She had a tulip named after her, the Angela Farmer.'

'Yes, but you said rose.'

'No, I didn't.'

'OK.'

Makepeace changed the subject.

'A doddle though, presumably?'

'Oh yes. The piece is half-written already, if I'm honest.'

He started fiddling with his string bags. 'I ought to check where she lives, I suppose, since I've got to arrange to get there on Monday,' he said, and distractedly pulled out a few scarves and Paris street-maps. 'I've got a diary in here somewhere.'

'More coffee?' asked Makepeace, and went to order it while Osborne delved among tangerines and library books, muttering, 'He said *rose*, though' several times under his breath.

'Ah, here we are.' The diary was found. 'Honiton,' he said.

'What?'

'Angela Farmer's address. Honiton in Devon.'

They looked at one another.

'You mean, like, Honiton where the nuts come from?'

'Oh, bugger. Bugger it, yes, I think I do.'

3

A hard day at the typesetters had left Tim pale and drawn. His big specs felt heavy on his face, and a deep weariness sapped his soul as he trudged back from the tube station with only a few minutes to spare before his Friday night curfew of half-past seven. Being the sort of chap who responds to pressure by withdrawing deeper and tighter into his own already shrink-wrapped body, Tim was often on Friday nights so tautly pulled together that he was actually on the verge of turning inside out. Not surprisingly, then, he carried himself pretty carefully for those last few yards to the front door. After all, the merest nudge in the right place, and *flip*! it might all be over.

It would be unfair to say, as many had, that Tim's outer coolness masked an inner coolness underneath. But peeling the layers off Tim was not a job many people could be bothered to undertake, especially since Tim did so little to encourage them. Once, when Tim was a small boy, he foolishly dug up some daffodil bulbs from his mother's flower-beds to see how they were doing (this was a favourite story of his ex-girlfriend Margaret, who thought it so funny she snorted like a pig when she told it). Well, it was Tim's great misfortune in life that nobody (including Margaret) had ever thought to dig him up in the same way, just to check that healthy growth was still a possibility.

Most people, then, considered Tim cool, aloof and just a bit of a geek (because of the specs). And that was it. To his own mother he was a daffodil murderer, a mystery never to be solved. To Margaret (a smug psychology graduate) he was a textbook obsessive. Only his cat, Lester, was really bothered to get better acquainted with him. But then, as the cynics will gladly tell you, any emotional cripple with a tin-opener is of devotional interest to his cat.

Today Tim was especially worried about the emotional turmoil ahead. A new proprietor, indeed – good grief, the whole thing spelt change, and he hated the sound of it. Textbook obsessives rarely disappoint in certain departments, and Tim was not the man to transgress the rules of an association. Thus, the past week had seen him dutifully fretting to the point of dizziness about the smallest of matters slipping from his control. The *Independent* had gone up by five pence! On Tuesday he had forgotten to change his desk calendar to the right day! Tonight he had trodden on an odd number of paving stones on his walk home from the tube! Tim never worried about things he could actually do something about – he never, for example, grew cross with the printers on Fridays, as Michelle did, when they were inefficient or lazy. But powerlessness made him frantic. The selling of the magazine to a new proprietor whose intentions were obscure – well, that was the kind of thing to drive him nuts.

It was with a genuine lack of enthusiasm that he unlocked the door to the flat. Since Margaret moved out, the place seemed spooky; he kept finding Margaret-shaped holes in its fabric. There were gaps in the bookshelves, empty drawers, an exactly half-filled bathroom cabinet, a clearly defined gap in the dust on the kitchen surface where her Magimix formerly stood. If he had been a sentimental person, he would have considered it sad. Nobody muttered 'For Pete's sake' when Tim checked the door for the fifth time before going to bed; nevertheless he heard the words not being spoken. Margaret's absence, to be honest, was more conspicuous to Tim than her presence had been. Sometimes, when he was changing the bed-linen, he had an awful feeling he would draw back the duvet and find a crude Margaret-shaped outline on the bottom sheet, like the ones the American cops draw around homicide victims on sidewalks.

The only thing she had left behind was the cat, a ginger tom with a loud purr, who wrecked Tim's attempts to work at home by ritually jumping up on every sheet of important paper (with wet paws), and then ceremoniously parking his bum on it. So Tim had stopped trying to work at home (which was a good thing). The only trouble was, he couldn't quite get the hang of feeding the cat at proper times, so that now, as Tim roved the dark, joyless flat turning on lights, Lester followed him about, making intense feed-me-Oh-God-feed-me noises combined with much unambiguous trouser-nudging. Tim shrugged distractedly and reached for a pad of sticky Post-it notes. FEED CAT, he wrote on the top sheet. This he peeled off and stuck to the nearest door-frame before continuing his perambulations.

As he moved into the hall he barely noticed that on every door-frame there were dozens of similar notes, slightly overlapping, as though left over from some jolly atavistic maypole ritual. He saw them, of course, because they were unmissable –

REMEMBER AUNTIE JOAN AT CHRISTMAS

DRY HAIR AFTER SHOWER

FEED CAT

JAMMY DODGERS ON OFFER AT PRICERIGHT

CHECK DOOR

FEED LESTER

TELL OSBORNE NOT TO WORRY ABOUT NEW EDITOR – SHEDS EVER GREEN

– he just didn't see anything odd.

Something a great deal more lively awaited Michelle when she too reached home that evening, at roughly the same hour. Mother – a nice-looking, grey-haired old woman in natty, mauve velour track-suit and trainers – was poised and ready in the darkened living-room, having planned the moment with the precision of a true enthusiast. Just as Michelle's key entered the lock, Mother tipped a number of smouldering cigarette butts on to the carpet around her wheelchair, pressed the button on the CD remote control (so that Irving Berlin's 'Always' began to play) and finally flung herself back in her seat – in what she hoped was an attitude of death from filial neglect. A momentary quandary about whether her eyes should be open or closed was hastily resolved, so that when Michelle burst into the room shouting, 'All right, all right, what is it this time?' she saw her mother's wide, staring eyeballs reflecting the little blue flames that were just beginning to reach up out of the Wilton.

There was artistry in it, undoubtedly, but Michelle had seen it before. Also, she could not help thinking – even as she stamped out the fire and switched off the music – that the gory hatchet-through-the-head accessory was slightly gilding the lily.

Meanwhile, in a nice living-room in south London, Osborne studied the expensive curtains (the words 'Very Peter Hall' came to mind, but he couldn't think why) and pondered the advantages of house-sitting as a way of life.

'House-sitting': how calm and steady it sounds. There is nothing steadier, after all, than a house; no posture more shock-resistant than sitting. Osborne, the man who sat in other people's sheds as a profession, also sat in other people's living-rooms when he went home. And as far as he was concerned, it was great, because it was cheap. The deal was, he stayed for free in other people's flats and watered their plants, while they took nice foreign holidays or worked abroad. People trusted him, it seemed; and then they recommended him to other people, who in turn gave him their keys and wrote him chummy notes about fish-food and window-locks, and afterwards overlooked the breakages. Osborne came with recommendations. He was easygoing and honest, though not particularly house-trained. Most people figured that, in a house-sitter, two out of three wasn't bad.

For the past few weeks he had been living in the home of an old journalist friend whose job had taken him to Los Angeles for six months. The Northern Line ran directly underneath this flat, and Osborne liked to listen to the trains rumbling in the tunnels far below. He had noticed that you could feel the tremor even outside on the busy street, and he liked it; it made him feel safe. But tonight he was rattled; for he had had a perplexing day. He could hardly believe, for one thing, that he had really sat helpless in the Birthplace of Aphrodite and agreed to let Makepeace come with him to Honiton on Monday (were they really going in *Makepeace's van?*). And worse than that, he seemed to remember saying that Makepeace could 'sit in' during the Angela Farmer interview. 'I'll just observe,' his friend had said. *What?* Since when was 'observing' such an innocuous activity? Observing counted as threatening behaviour. The thought of Makepeace observing made him almost want to cry.

Taking refuge in food, Osborne popped along to the kitchen with the intention of knocking up a tasty meal, an intention which (if nothing else) paid tribute to hope's triumph over experience, since Osborne had never succeeded in creating a tasty meal in his life. Recipe books scared him, especially when they had jaunty titles such as *One is Fun!*, so his usual method was to open a few tins of things left behind by the absent home-owner – some tinned spaghetti, say, and a slab of tuna – and mix it up in a bowl, with prunes for afters. This he would place on a tray with a glass of expensive cognac from a bottle found stashed behind the gas meter, and then eat in front of the TV.

Osborne entertained few qualms about helping himself to the stuff people left behind in cupboards. Being unacquainted with the notion of housekeeping, he assumed that food and booze just sort of belonged in the house and should be used accordingly. Only once had he encountered hostility to this view, when he pointed out to a returning home-owner that her supply of toilet paper had run out halfway through his six-month stay. He had been obliged to buy some more, he said, the full astonishment of the experience still making him shake his head in disbelief. The woman in question, brown and dusty from six months' fending for herself in the Australian outback (with no Andrex supplier within a thousand miles), took this news by merely gaping and gesticulating, speechless.

It was hard to imagine interviewing someone with Makepeace listening in. 'The maestro at work,' Makepeace had said, with an insinuating smile. Was this man mad, or what? Osborne had certainly done some good stuff in his time (the David Essex, as aforementioned, was unsurpassable), but methodology was not his strong point, heaven knew. Osborne was convinced that Makepeace merely wanted to expose him; what other motive could he have? He imagined the scene: himself pretending to consult his notes while panicking what to ask next, Angela Farmer croaking 'You OK, honey?' and handing him a clean tissue for the sweat dribbling in his eyes, and Makepeace stepping in with some smart-arse brilliant question and hijacking the whole enterprise. Bluffing was hard work at any time, without being watched.

Twiddling some cold Heinz spaghetti on a spoon, he looked up to see that Angela Farmer, by some happy coincidence, was on the television screen right this minute, in her new smash-hit sitcom *Forgive Us Our Trespasses As We Forgive Those Who Trespass Against Us*. He could hardly believe his good fortune. 'Blimey, *research*,' he remarked aloud, with his mouth full, 'that's a bit of luck.' In the old days, of course, when he was young and keen, he would have looked for Angela Farmer's name in the reference books, got some cuttings from a newspaper library, swotted up, requested tapes from the BBC Press Office. But these days he reckoned that a chance sighting of his subject on the box was quite sufficient to be going on with. A person's curriculum vitae, he had discovered, rarely had much bearing on their relationship with the shed.

'Nice-looking woman,' he said, and got up to look at her more closely. 'Makepeace is right, she's great.' But then, as he got closer to the screen, he suddenly felt all weightless again – and it wasn't the prunes, because he hadn't eaten them yet. 'Don't I *know* you?' he said, and peered at Angela Farmer more closely still. 'I do, don't I? I know you from somewhere.' But of course she didn't enlighten him. She was on the telly, after all.

The sitcom was a humdrum affair (as so many are) in which Ms Farmer played a wisecracking New Yorker called Eve, opposite a limp-wristed British aristo named Adam. Osborne checked the title again in the paper – *Forgive Us Our*

Trespasses – and decided not to worry too deeply about this interesting confusion of Old and New Testaments, because it was probably the product of ignorance rather than design. Adam was played by another famous TV star (in whose sparkling greenhouse it had once been Osborne's privilege to feel sweat in his eyes); and the idea of the piece was that Adam and Eve did not get on. That was all. The remarkable serendipity of their names was oddly never remarked on, although the title sequence did show an animated naked couple enveloped by a serpent and dithering over a pound of Coxes. What a shame, thought Osborne, that 'Lead Us Not into Temptation' had already been snapped up by that game show on ITV, and that this Adam-and-Eve vehicle had nothing to do with original sin (or trespass) in any case. But the audience seemed to like it. They laughed like drains every twenty seconds or so, whenever Eve and Adam had another hilarious collision of wills.

'Milk or lemon?' a hotel waiter would ask.

'Milk,' piped Adam; 'Lemon,' barked Eve (both speaking simultaneously); *Hargh, hargh, hargh*, went the audience.

But Osborne had stopped listening to the dialogue and had even abandoned the delights of his Tuna Surprise; he was peering at the snarling close-ups of Angela Farmer with an increasing unease, his initial frisson of recognition having broadened and deepened until it flowed through his body like a river and leaked out horribly at his toes.

'Inside or outside?'

'In,' said Adam; 'Out,' said Eve; and the audience roared again.

Osborne felt ill. Had she said '*Out*'? Where had he heard her say 'Out' like that? Perhaps it was his imagination, but he suddenly felt quite certain he had heard Angela Farmer say 'Out' in that pointed manner before. And the horrible thing was, she must have said it to *him*.

Back at Tim's flat, *Forgive Us Our Trespasses* was also playing. There wasn't much on the other channels that evening. But in any case, *Forgive Us* was the sort of television Tim particularly enjoyed: safe, predictable, and OK if you missed bits when suddenly you felt the urge to check that the fridge light still worked. Watching Eve with interest, he found that he rather envied Osborne's luck in interviewing Ms Farmer; he must ask him what she was really like, beyond the parameters of the shed stuff. He reached for a Post-it pad and wrote TELL OSBORNE I THINK A.F. IS A V. FINE ACTRESS, and stuck the label on the side of the coffee-table.

Lester made a noise that sounded like 'meat' (but it might have been 'me, eat'), and arched his back before sinking his front claws into the chair and ripping. Teatime was long past, yet the happy clink of spoon on cat-bowl was yet to be heard, and Lester was running out of hints. Why was Tim so oblivious to feline nuance? It was enough to drive a cat crackers. So it was back to ripping the sofa, even though he didn't really feel like it. 'How banal, really,' thought Lester, as he dug in, and the fabric made *poc, poc, poc-opoc-poc* noises, like fireworks on Chinese New Year. 'How stupid.'

'Just stop that!' said Tim in a voice so loud and commanding that Lester sprang back and gave him a look. Tim stirred in his chair, but Lester was right not to race to the kitchen, for it was a false alarm. Tim reached for his pad again. BE MORE PATIENT WITH LESTER, he wrote, and, at a loss where to put it, stuck it on the cat.

Makepeace sat at his typewriter, not watching the TV, and composed the covering letter for his *Come Into the Garden* book review, every word of which was an obvious lie to anyone who knew him.

Dear Tim [*he wrote; actually this part not a lie exactly, but read on*],

Sorry [*not at all*] you did not receive this by fax on Thursday as requested, but as I explained on the phone I faxed it from the copy shop [*no, he didn't*] and then lost my original while gardening [*stretching it a bit here, but there you are*]. So I have retyped this from notes [*yawn*] and hope you like it. I actually think it came out better the second time! [*clever touch this, the maestro at work, as it were*].

Funny, I agree, that we didn't bump into one another at the launch of the Fruit Garden books last week [*he wasn't there*]. I was definitely there [*see previous note*]! In fact, I looked high and low for you, but couldn't see you [*classic turning of tables; never fails to convince*].

All the best,

M. Makepeace

Miles eastward along the river, past Greenwich Reach and the Isle of Dogs, Lillian was sitting with her feet up watching *Forgive Us Our Trespasses*, just like everybody else. From the steamy kitchen she could hear the pleasant sounds of George (the hubby) making dinner, and she looked up in proper feeble-invalid fashion to see him present her with a pre-prandial cup-soup, made especially in her favourite Bunnykins mug. Some people might balk at the idea of cup-soups forming any part of an evening meal, but somehow it had become part of the routine. The idea was that, with God's help of course, it would keep up Lillian's strength until the arrival of solid food.

'Dwarling,' he said in a singsong baby voice. (I'm sorry if this is ghastly, but it's true.) Lillian looked up, saw the cup-soup, pretended it was all a big surprise and gave him a sweet, affected, little-girl look that was enough honestly to freeze the blood of any disinterested onlooker. She peered into the bunny-mug and frowned a deep frown.

'No cru-tongs, bunny,' she lisped, her mouth turned down in disappointment.

'Poor bunny,' agreed her husband (who by day, incidentally, was a used-car salesman). 'No cru-tongs for bunnywunny.'

He hung his head, extended his arms behind his back and kicked his instep.

Fortunately, she smiled her forgiveness, and the moment of conflict passed. Otherwise there might have been a tantrum. But tonight they made secret-society gestures with their little fingers, as proof that the no-crutong incident had been forgotten. Don't ask. They just seemed to enjoy it, that's all.

'Bunny tired?' asked Mister Bunny, after a pause.

'Bunny *werry* tired.'

'Did the phone never stop ringing again?'

'Never.' Lillian pouted and delicately picked some fluff off her teddy-slippers, real tears of childish anguish starting in her eyes.

'Phone went ring ring ring ring ring ring –'

'Poor bunny, with phone going ring.'

'Yes, poor bunny.'

'Nice spinach for tea, make bunny stwong.'

'Bunny *never* be stwong, bunny.'

'I know,' said Mister Bunny, with a tinge of heart-felt regret. 'Poor poor bunny-wunny.'

'Mmm,' said Lillian, closing her eyes.

Osborne was trying to make notes for his interview on Tuesday, but somehow the usual all-purpose questions about sheds looked rather hollow and unsatisfactory: 'Old shed/new shed? Shed important/unimportant? Hose kept in shed? Or not? (Any funny hose anecdotes?)'

He looked at the TV screen and there she was again, this

amazing blonde woman with the mystery and the scarifying attitude.

'Singles or double?' asked a hotel receptionist.

'Double,' said Adam; 'Singles,' barked Eve.

It was the last line of the show, and Osborne switched off just before the inevitable gale of appreciative studio applause. Looking at his notebook, he saw he had written: 'Bugger the trespasses and bugger the shed. Why didn't you tell me who you were?' And now he looked at it, aghast, because he didn't have a clue what it meant.

Michelle heard the closing music to *Forgive Us Our Trespasses* from the kitchen, where she had just discovered a cache of trick daggers and tomato ketchup wedged behind the U-bend in the cupboard under the sink. She felt a twinge tired of all this, though far be it from her, etcetera. Nobody at the office knew about Mother; it was such a sad old commonplace for a single professional woman to have a loony mum at home that she simply wouldn't stand for anyone to know, especially not Lillian; she wanted to circle the offending cliché in thick blue pen and send it back for a rewrite. But life is not susceptible to sub-editing, by and large, and the mad mum remained fast embedded in Michelle's text. Mother was a liability – mischievous, hurtful and addicted to practical jokes. Underneath the sink Michelle found an invoice, too: evidently Mother's latest consignment from her favourite mail-order novelty company included a new severed hand which had not yet come to light.

She sat back on her heels for a moment and, without undue self-pity, considered what she had to put up with. The irony was unbearable. Here she was, possibly the only person in the world who knew the difference between 'forbear' and 'forebear', and she was also the only person of her acquaintance who was consistently obliged to put both words together in the same sentence.

Tim made a note, WATCH FORGIVE US OUR TRESPS NEXT FRIDAY DON'T FORGET, and attached it to his jumper with a safety-pin, next to GO TO BED AT SOME POINT – which he had written carefully backwards, to be read when he caught sight of himself in a mirror.

Lillian and Mister Bunny pulled faces at one another, trays on their laps, and affected diddums-y thoughts as the credits rolled. (I'm sorry.)

'Dat wath qw' goo',' said Mister Bunny.

'Mmm,' said Lillian, 'but this spinach was gooder!'

Makepeace wrote another letter, beginning with the words 'Can't understand how this did not reach you by post, although I wonder now whether your secretary gave me the correct address.' He noted without pleasure that he could type this particular sentence as quickly as he could do 'The quick brown fox jumps over the lazy dog.'

Angela Farmer switched off the TV and consulted her diary. 'Oh yeah,' she remarked to no one in particular, 'the schmuck from the gardening magazine. I suppose I better mention the goddam tulip.'

And Lester the cat, festooned with Post-it notes, made his way to the darkened kitchen, knocked a tin of Turkey Whiskas to the floor, and rolled it carefully with his nose and paws in the general direction of the living-room. If that stupid bastard fails to get the hint this time, he thought, I'll scream.

4

The magazine for which all these people worked was a modest weekly publication, usually running to thirty-two or forty pages, with a circulation of around twenty thousand. In its far off post-war heyday – which none of the present staff could remember – it had achieved a sale four times greater, but during the sixties, seventies and eighties its appeal had dipped, declined and finally levelled out; and today it would not be unkind to say that in the broad mental landscape of the average British newsagent, *Come Into the Garden* was virtually invisible to the naked eye.

This vanishing act represented a great lost opportunity. Gardening had become a lot more sexy in the past ten years, the garden centre had almost supplanted the supermarket as a magnet for disposable dosh, and the urgent question of morally defensible peat substitutes had become the staple talk of middle-class dinner tables; yet *Come Into the Garden* still somehow failed to clean up. Michelle was often struck by the sad image of her beloved magazine pathetically sheltering indoors in the breezy climate of the 1980s while other, brighter, glossier monthly publications came stumping heartily into its territory, utterly oblivious to its existence. She imagined these competitors taking a quick glance round, sniffing the wind, and then digging energetically with flashy stainless steel implements, heedlessly scattering the sod.

Michelle's picture did not end there, either. It was remarkably colourful and detailed. For example, *Come Into the Garden* wore a pair of brown corduroys, tied at the knee with string, and an old jumper with holes, and plimsolls, while the rivals were togged in Barbour jackets, riding boots and aristocratic flat caps, rather like the pictures of Captain Mark Phillips in *Hello!* magazine. Michelle was good at mental pictures. Once, when she observed Lillian standing tall, knock-kneed, spare-tyred and stupid in the middle of the office, the word 'Ostrich!' leapt quite unbidden to her mind, and she had relished the analogy ever since. She had successfully thought of other animal-types for the remainder of her colleagues, too. But luckily – apart from flinging the odd 'Oink, oink' noise at a departing back – she kept this personal taxonomy to herself.

The depressing thing about working for *Come Into the Garden*, however, was not the variety of wildlife. It was that the general public had this awful habit of remembering it from years ago, placing it on the same conceptual shelf as *Reveille*, the *Daily Sketch*, Noggin the Nog and Harold Macmillan. 'Blimey,' they said, shaking their heads in disbelief, 'my *Nan* used to read that; is it really still going?' – at which one could only smile weakly and try not to take offence. It was nobody's fault, this widely held assumption that *Come Into the Garden* had long since sought eternal peace in the great magazine rack in the sky. Nevertheless, it required strength of character for those intimately acquainted with the title not to take such comments personally. After all, it was a bit like being accused repeatedly of outliving your own obituary, or being dead but not lying down.

Imagine the difficulty of applying for other jobs. Michelle in particular had tried quite strenuously to outgrow *Come Into the Garden*, but she had been compelled to realize that citing her occupation as chief sub of this magazine sounded suspiciously like Coronation Programme Seller, or Great Fire of London Damage Assessor: prospective employers simply assumed she hadn't worked for years. On the whole she bitterly envied the sensible, big-headed young journalists who had joined the title only to use it as a tiny stepping-stone en route to bigger things. They had come into the garden (as it were) and then pissed right off again, with no regrets, and moreover without a trace of loam on their fancy shoes. She did not blame them for this, she just despised them – a feeling she expressed quite eloquently by affecting never to have heard of them ('Paul *who*? Doesn't ring any bells') whenever their names were raised.

Editors too had come and gone, almost on a seasonal basis, but that wasn't so bad, because mostly they kept themselves to themselves. And if they tried anything clever, Lillian was a highly effective means of damage control, since she paid absolutely no attention to anything they asked her to do. At the time of this story – the early 1990s – *Come Into the Garden* had seen four editors in five years, but it would be fair to say that 'seeing' was literally the limit of the acquaintance. A police line-up featuring all four of them would not necessarily elicit a flicker of recognition. By now, the long-standing staffers had grown quite blasé about meeting new bosses – content merely to count them in and then count them all out again. Indeed, when this dull Mainwaring chap (James? John?) had first settled his ample bum into the editor's chair in July, Lillian had asked him straight off, day one, what sort of thing he fancied for a leaving present, on the principle that it would save awkwardness later on.

Lillian thrived on the chaos of mismanagement. Half the time she had no boss at all (and she refused to work for anyone besides the editor), and the other half she could spend in playing lucky dip with the post-bag, or aggressively blocking the paths of busy, timid people (such as Tim) with sudden rockfalls of inane chat. Lillian's behaviour was quite easy to predict, by the way, once you realized she was talkative in inverse proportion to the amount of talk anyone cared to hear at that particular moment. It was an infallible gift. Thus, when she was asked to disseminate important news, she automatically clammed up, kept her counsel, went home, phoned in sick next day. Whereas when everyone was bustling, agitated and far too busy to listen, she did the famous Ancient Mariner impression, expertly mooring them to the spot with heavy verbal anchors about sod all.

'Oh, *look!*' she would announce to no one in particular, flapping an envelope in her tongs too fast for anyone to see what it was. 'Someone's written to Mike McCarthy!'

She would look around to see what effect this was having. And she would know, with the instinct of a top professional, that the sullen, negative take-up (people staring at walls, and so on) meant she actually had the room in the palm of her hand.

'But don't you see? Mike McCarthy left ages ago!'

At this point young Tim might rashly attempt to tiptoe past, but be tugged forcibly to a halt by tight invisible chains.

'You *must* remember Mike McCarthy, Tim!' she shrieked. 'He was the editor who tried to do away with the "Dear Donald" page, just because his name wasn't Donald! For heaven's sake. I kept telling him, didn't I, *nobody's* name is Donald!'

And not for the first time, Tim would wriggle miserably, like bait on a hook, and think how clever Ulysses had been, in the old story, to lash himself to a mast, with ear-plugs.

That Tim did not remember Mike McCarthy, Lillian knew full well. Tim had been deputy editor for only a year, and had taken the job straight from a postgraduate journalism course. In fact, at the time of Mike McCarthy's ill-fated editorship, Tim had still been a quiet bespectacled schoolboy dreaming of a career modelled on Norman Mailer's, and wondering how his myopia, general weediness and night-time emissions would affect his chance of success. But it was Tim's newness, more than his youth, that put him at a disadvantage where Lillian was concerned, despite the fact he had done more for the magazine in a year than she had done since *circa* 1978. Michelle and Lillian had come into the garden long before everyone else, and the length of their stay was an accomplishment for which they both demanded a high level of respect. At the all-too-frequent leaving parties – for the transient editor (or whoever) whose nugatory role in the magazine's forty-year history was ruthlessly scratched from the record the moment he hit the pavement outside ('Mike *who*? I don't recall') – the heroic span of Lillian and Michelle was usually trotted out again, mainly because it was the one single topic either of them could be persuaded to talk about in company.

For people with so little in common, it was noticeable how much Michelle and Lillian made comparisons with one another. True, they were the same age, forty-two; they had both worked at *Come Into the Garden* for fifteen years; and neither could stick being in the same room with the other. But that was it; these were the only points at which their experience coincided. On this crucial length-of-service issue, in fact, Michelle could *just* remember life before Lillian, in that same wistful glimpse-of-yesterday's-sunshine sort of way that some people can *just* remember being happy before the war, or sex before Aids, or global innocence before the Bomb. And when asked politely by craven sub-editors about the changes she had seen (at those godforsaken leaving parties amid the crisps and sausage rolls), Michelle was good at saying, with her eyes fixed musingly on the ceiling, 'Well, funnily enough *I can* just remember life before Lillian,' pronouncing the words with such perfectly judged emphasis that everyone latched on to the war-Aids-and-Bomb analogy without it ever being openly stated.

Come Into the Garden was a miserable, inert place to work, no doubt about it. Osborne's joy in turning up once a week to soak up the atmosphere was a measure of his desperation, nothing more. This was the sort of office where the plants embraced easeful death like an old friend, the stationery cupboard gave a wild, disordered suggestion of marauders on horseback, and nobody washed the coffee cups until the bacterial cultures had grown so active they could be seen performing push-ups and forward-rolls. There is a theory that says if employees have few outside distractions (i.e. don't have much of a home-life), they will make the most of work, but in the case of *Come Into the Garden* the opposite appeared to be true. Miserable at home meant dismal all round. The words 'Get a life!' were once hurled at an affronted Michelle by a fly-by-night sub as he stalked out one day at the typesetters, never to return. It was a brutal thing to say (the other subs exchanged significant glances before silently dividing the recreant's bun), yet nobody could deny it was an accurate assessment of the problem.

For Michelle's self-sacrifice was an appalling trap, with glaringly few personal compensations. And unfortunately it affected everyone, because she measured commitment by the yardstick of her own strict voluntary martyrdom. People resented this; it put them in a no-win situation. Besides the sub-editors under Michelle's control whom we have heard about, there were four colleagues with status equal or superior to hers – art editor (Marian), features editor (Mark), advertising manager (Toby) and deputy editor (Tim) – all of whom periodically took grave offence at Michelle's continual assertion that she cared a hundred times more about the magazine than they could possibly do. 'No, no, you go home, Tim,' she would say. 'Why should you hang around? I know how you love *Inspector Morse*. Leave everything to me. I'm usually here until half-past nine anyway. I've been here for fifteen years, don't forget; I ought to be used to it by now!'

Michelle's big mistake was to suppose she had no illusions. Just because she had seen a few dozen colleagues come and go, loam-free, and had sub-edited several hundred celebrity interviews about sheds (in which Osborne did indeed make all the sheds sound the same), she thought she had seen it all. But alas, she was wrong. A lifetime of rewriting 'Me and My Shed' was not the worst hand fate could deal you, not by a long chalk. What she was yet to discover, as she sat on the kitchen floor on that Friday night with only the unknown whereabouts of Mother's trick severed hand to disturb her mind, was that James Mainwaring (or *was* it John?) had already been declared the last editor of *Come Into the Garden*. The last *ever*, that is. If all went according to plan, those anxious readers who had phoned about 'Build your own greenhouse' had been absolutely right to worry: they would soon be left high and dry with a stack of panes and a lot of wet putty on their hands. And *Come Into the Garden*, for all the sacrifice it had wrung from Michelle, would return to the earth from which it came; ashes to ashes, compost to compost, dust to dust. No one at *Come Into the Garden* would survive to say 'Michelle *who?*' some day; nothing would remain.

For while she knew that the publishers, Wm Frobisher, had sold the title along with its lucrative seaside postcards business to an extremely youthful entrepreneur in the West Country, she did not yet know that the said young whippersnapper had decided immediately to close it down, merely retaining the Victoria premises of *Come Into the Garden* for his own personal headquarters. She did not know that the typesetters and printers had already been contacted by the whippersnapper's solicitors; or that a personal letter to each of the staff was already sitting on the whippersnapper's breakfast nook, awaiting signature. The little upstart had already inspected the building with his dad, in fact, and the spooky truth was that he had taken one look at Michelle's little corner and earmarked it immediately as the proposed position for his own executive desk. He had even helped himself to one of her Extra Strong Mints and admired her range of nail varnish.

Come Into the Garden was nothing like paradise, and never had been. But being cast out of it was going to be a pretty grisly business.

The decision to close *Come Into the Garden*, by the way, had taken only a few seconds.

'Dad,' said young Gordon, 'I've bought this old magazine. What do you think?' Frobisher's had sent Gordon a few recent issues, with a compliments slip.

'What's it called?'

'*Come Into the Garden.*'

'Never.'

'No, that's right.'

'Blimey,' said Gordon's dad, turning it over in his hands. 'Your Nan used to read this, when I was little. I can't believe it's still going.'

And that was it.

Gordon Clarke, at nineteen, was a red-headed, freckly prodigy of the computer software business; his father a nice-looking, broad-shouldered ex-fireman running a pleasant B&B. They were good people, Gordon and his dad, and considering their recent soaring fortunes, not a bit flash. Devon was their adopted home, the family having been transplanted from south London when Gordon was ten. Gordon had grown up knowing how to make a bed in three and a half minutes and carry four cooked breakfasts without a tray; apart from that, however, he was no better equipped for a managing directorship than most boys of his age. Given this background, then, Gordon's acquaintance with magazine publishing was scarcely intimate; and his concern for the continued job security of a bunch of anonymous deadbeat journalists on a dusty old magazine like *Come Into the Garden* was bound to be in the rough vicinity of nil.

His phenomenal early success he owed to a computer game invented in the wonderful summer of 1986, which he had named *Digger*. It had made him a teenage millionaire and a darling of feature-writers everywhere. In fact, if Osborne had only been more alert to the happenings of the world in general, he would have been down to interview Gordon's shed. The idea of *Digger* was simple: it used the principles of the traditional treasure hunt, mixed it up with some significant ancient legend and some primitive three-dimensional virtual reality, and somehow caught the public's attention so utterly that, overnight, the Digger became a fashionable figure for the first time since the seventeenth century. 'Where's young Jason?' spinster aunties would say on visits to family homes. 'Oh, he's upstairs *digging*,' would be the apparently meaningless reply. It was one of those instances where the new meaning of a word almost supplants the old, so that blokes heading for their allotments with shovels over their shoulders were obliged to explain to their kiddies what kind of digging exactly they were referring to.

Not surprisingly, Gordon's position at the cutting edge of the games software business was itself usurped, in time, by even younger tykes with even fancier ideas, but by then he had made a decent fortune from *Digger* and had listened to the advice of his wise old dad, with the result that he now controlled a modest, diversified business empire, with leisure as its loosely connecting thread, and a break-even B&B in Honiton as its base. His dad sometimes lamented that Gordon's mum had not lived to see it all – but Gordon did not mind so very much. His mum had died when he was a baby; and anyway he adored his dad. His main concern at the moment, in fact, was that, if Digger Enterprises moved to London, his dad would be left behind to run the B&B alone, a thought he could hardly bear.

One of the ingenious features of *Digger*, much remarked upon by adult observers of the game, was that the player sometimes dug up stuff that looked like gold, only to find that it stuck to his hands and afflicted him with debilitating pain and anguish. Gordon's classical education was not extensive, but he knew about the Midas touch, and had also been horrified as a child by the story of Hercules and the shirt of Nessus, so he had simply put the two ideas together. *Digger* devotees (as well as Gordon's many interviewers) had often pointed out the maturity of his moral insight, and posed the obvious poor-little-rich-boy question of whether Gordon himself might have dug up more than he could handle. Would the unexpected wealth turn sour? Gordon's generally cheerful disposition gave the lie to this idea, but it had certainly struck him lately that the possible separation from his dad would be just the thing to make him rue the day of *Digger's* success.

It was his Auntie Angela who offered him the best advice on the subject of success. 'Expect to lose all the pals of your ba-zoom, Gordon,' she warned him flatly on the day *Digger* came out (Gordon was fourteen and motherless, as aforementioned). 'Auntie' Angela (no relation) was American, with a house just up the road. She sharpened a cracked fingernail briskly with an emery board and took a deep drag on a cigarette, with the effect of turning her already dry-throated delivery to pure essence of razor-blade. 'Listen, Gordon baby,' she snarled, 'it is harder for a camel to thread a needle with its goddam *eye* than for a friend to forgive you success. Okay?' She was a bit of a dragon sometimes, Auntie Angela, toughened by years of working in light comedy on British television, her skin tanned to a leathery yellow hide by decades of sun and cigarettes. But although she breathed fire and snorted smoke, she was not alarming to Gordon; he basked in the warm ashes like a fledgling phoenix not sure whether to rise up flapping or snuggle down for a bit more cosy snooze. Science, by the way, had not yet revealed the full perils of passive smoking.

As Gordon remembered it, this important conversation took place one sunny afternoon in Angela's shed; the same shed that Osborne and Makepeace were planning (as you will long since have guessed) to visit for *Come Into the Garden* in a couple of days' time. Thinking back, Gordon could visualize the smoke and dust hanging in equal density in a shaft of sunlight from the small window; he could see Angela's stacks of yellowing sheet music mixed in with the pots and trowels, and he could smell the earthy bulb fibre in its bag. He had spent many happy afternoons in that shed, actually, with Angela narrating the plots of Broadway musicals for his delight, and belting out all the songs by way of illustration. He was particularly fond of *Showboat* – especially 'Just My Bill' and 'I Still Likes Me'.

So for now all was rosy in Gordon's particular world. He played football on Sundays, made visits to Angela, reaped ever-increasing royalties on *Digger* and kept up with the latest research into the technology of virtual reality. He was a genius, of course; but not a bit overbearing with it. He seemed to have the enviable capacity of enjoying his good fortune; a talent that the profile writers, after consulting child psychologists, had deduced at length to have a rather banal explanation – viz., that he owed it to a lifetime of 'proper parenting'. Really. One of these psychologists used an analogy which would almost have endeared Gordon to readers of *Come Into the Garden* (if he weren't just about to close down their magazine): she said that Gordon had had the luck of being 'planted in a soil that nourished him'; a luck, she went on to say, that was as rare as a snowdrop in August.

And the luck was still with him, because her comment prompted him to think of a new virtual reality program, which he now hugged to himself, for he knew it would revolutionize the whole leisure-perception-Gameboy business and place the name of Gordon Clarke on the rollcall of history, along with Newton and Buddha, and Rodgers and Hammerstein. Because in this new virtual reality program, the player would not vanquish opponents or dig for treasure, but would *feel himself grow.* Just by strapping a computer-generated visual world on to his bonce, he would experience an unfurling, an expanding, a reaching towards the light – like a snowdrop, a yucca plant or a mighty oak, depending on preference.

Gordon's provisional title for it was *Phototropism* (though he suspected this might have to change), and his ambitions for it were boundless. Imagine returning to the real, warped, stunted world after an experience such as *Phototropism*! It would be like reporting back from heaven; it could change people for ever.

Meanwhile *Come Into the Garden* does well to shelter indoors from the harsh pelting weather sweeping towards it from the west. No point getting the corduroys damp in a misplaced effort to stay the inevitable. Its demise will be significant only to a small number of people – and, being mostly gardening types, the readers are well acquainted with the ruthless survivalist principles of pruning, dead-heading and plucking out anything that's got a bit rusty round the edges. In short, they will be cross, but ultimately they will understand. But still, one can't help feeling sorry for the poor old mag as it waits unawares for its sudden end. It has no idea it has done anything wrong. It thinks it has permanent roots; it thinks it's a perennial. And it even expects Osborne and Makepeace to hit the road next Monday and bring back a 'Me and My Shed' so brilliant, witty and generally wildly glorious that it will make the whole world of gardening journalism sit up and say, 'Wow.' Which just goes to show how out of touch it really is.

5

'I love this van,' said Makepeace, as he accelerated the old Fiesta away from the kerb with a screech of tyres and punched a few buttons on the crackly radio cassette so that a loud Dire Straits number drilled the air. Osborne, tightly duffled in his coat and fastened securely in his seat belt, clutched his overnight bag hard against his chest and, with his head thrown sharply back by the G-force of the take-off, prayed silently with his eyes closed to the patron saint of hopeless causes. But an immediate squeal, thunk and shout forced him to look up. Makepeace had belatedly noticed a large coach bearing down on them and braked, just in time, to a violent dead stop.

It was an ominous beginning. The van rocked furiously on its chassis, and Makepeace's push-bike shot forward from its position in the rear so that a hurtling handlebar struck Osborne quite forcibly on the back of the head. The sound of *tring!* is not usually associated with despair, but there is a first time for everything. Makepeace, incensed, grabbed his door handle, evidently with the intention of leaping out to defend his affronted honour, but fortunately the offending coach roared off in a haze of exhaust, because otherwise a rendezvous for pistols at dawn would surely have been appointed.

'Pillock,' averred Makepeace, turning the music a little louder. 'Arsehole.' At which the van lurched off again, this time (by an undeserved stroke of good fortune) locating a perfectly Fiesta-sized gap in the stream of westward rush hour traffic.

Devon had never seemed further off than it did now to Osborne, as he contemplated London's South Circular Road and imagined the grim prospect of his friend taking up cudgels for his legendary infallibility every six or seven yards between Putney and Stonehenge. 'I did *not* pull out without indicating'; 'But you did'; 'I did *not*, you arsehole'; 'You did, you fucking maniac'; 'Take off those glasses and say that'; *Biff!*; 'Aagh!'; *Boff! Tinkle! Tring!* If debate over traffic accidents tends to bring out aggression in people, Makepeace had just the right demeanour of overweening smugness to invite a nasty smack in the eye from virtually any fellow motorist not laid low by infirmity or disqualified from punch-ups by gender or divine ordinance. Mind you, come to think of it, 'Take off that wimple and say that' sounded pretty feasible, too.

Osborne suddenly realized he couldn't remember why he liked this bloke. 'Do we need to fill up?' he yelled above the din of music and engine, but his words were ignored. Shortly afterwards, however, Makepeace announced to no one in particular, 'Hey, *I'd* better get some *petrol*,' and swerved into a garage, narrowly missing a woman on crutches with a baby on her back.

It is a misplaced perception tragically common among neurotics that dangerous situations are somehow not dangerous *per se*, but are merely sent to try them. Famous for worrying about nothing, the Osbornes of this world paradoxically respond to genuinely scary situations by affecting not to notice, because somehow it makes them feel better. So, while any normal person might have sprung from Makepeace's van at this perfect opportunity, pretending all of a sudden to remember a valid train ticket in the back of their wallet,

Osborne merely breathed deeply, glanced around to check that the crutch lady was still vertical, and reached into his bag for the solace of the packed lunch.

'Cup cake?' he said. Makepeace applied the handbrake and stared at his passenger in surprise, as though Osborne had been deliberately keeping his presence a secret. He repeated the offer. 'Er, cup cake, Makepeace?' 'Certainly not,' said the master of all their fates. 'For God's sake, can't you see I'm driving?'

An hour later, as the little yellow van screamed and rattled from the M3 on to the old West Country road, and the surrounding Hampshire scenery presented its quaint palette of November greens and browns, Osborne brushed the last of the chocolate crumbs off his lap, feeling obscurely pleased. He was, when all was said and done, a man who took his consolations where he found them, and experience had taught him there were few situations that did not contain them if you looked hard enough. So, Number One, he had survived this miserable journey thus far with only a slight bash to the head; and Number Two, eight cup cakes in a single sitting was a personal best. He noted with additional satisfaction that in six cases out of the eight, he had so carefully peeled the silver paper that no chocolate icing had been caught in the little corrugations. So, not so bad, really. Now he leaned back, tried to blot out the FM babble of the radio (the signal was wandering, but Makepeace didn't notice), and closed his eyes so that Makepeace's maverick tendency to thunder up close behind other cars and then scarily overtake on the left was something he merely felt in his gut rather than experienced fully through the organs of vision.

Riding as a passenger in Makepeace's van was in one

regard quite different from what he had expected: there was apparently no necessity for talk. In other ways, alas, it was precisely what he might have imagined. Makepeace's driving was of the God-I'm-dying-for-a-pee school: fast, tense and involved, and with his torso inclined so far forward in his seat that occasionally his nose bumped against the windscreen, leaving a smear of grease. Osborne felt no compulsion to communicate, therefore, especially since Makepeace's few utterances were exclusively addressed either to road signs (whose information he predictably refused to believe), or to other motorists (who thankfully could not respond). 'Since when?' was an evident favourite in Makepeace's open-road repertoire ('Basingstoke "four miles"? Oh yes? *Since when?*'). Osborne guessed rightly that this was a question that required no answer – or at least none that he was in any position to supply.

So instead he turned his mind to the mystery of Angela Farmer, whose part in his downfall he was still agonizingly unable to place, despite the automatic writing he had seen on his notepad on Friday night. 'Why didn't you tell me who you were?' it had said ominously, with a kind of low cello vibrato – reminding Osborne of something from a sensational nineteenth-century novel, along the lines of 'Gone! And never called me mother,' or, 'But there is one thing no one has ever told you, my pretty; you are mad, quite mad.' For a man who treasured the quietness and regularity of his life, and was convinced he had never paddled in the shallows of melodrama, this mystery was cause only for alarm. What a shame, he grimaced, that all the cup cakes had gone. Chocolate is always so helpful when a man wants to think.

It was at this point, unfortunately, that Makepeace decided to get chatty. Thirty miles from Hyde Park Corner, he suddenly relaxed with an audible sigh. He leaned back in his seat, switched off the radio, lowered his speed and altered his entire disposition. 'So,' he said, 'tell me what you reckon to this Angela Farmer.'

For a moment, Osborne was so surprised to find himself addressed that he glanced into the back of the van to find out who Makepeace was talking to, and received the full force of a handlebar just below his eye.

'Ouch,' he said. 'Who, me?'

'Mm. What angle are you going to take?'

'I don't know.' Osborne hated being asked questions about his work; his answers always sounded so unconvincing. 'I haven't got one.'

'Course you have.' Makepeace apparently knew all about it. 'You can't do an interview without an *angle.*'

Osborne, a man who had never had an angle in his life, and wasn't sure he would recognize one if it snuggled in beside him in the Fiesta, shrugged and consulted his notes, faintly hoping that a heading marked 'Angle' would appear miraculously at the top. It didn't.

'No. Really,' he said. 'I just thought I'd ask about the shed.'

His friend laughed scornfully, as though he were pulling his leg.

'You don't mean that.'

'I do.'

Osborne felt he was being got at. Which of course he was.

'All right, you do,' conceded Makepeace. 'But there must be some sort of idea of what you want her to say before you start, surely. I mean, what do you usually ask? Tell me how it goes.'

Osborne sighed. He hated this.

'Well, it varies from person to person,' he said at last. 'Sometimes they say do I want to see the shed on my own, and then talk about it indoors over a drink or something, which saves them the bother of coming out; and sometimes we go down together, which I prefer actually, because I find it leads to the best stories.'

'Right.' Makepeace noisily dropped a gear to overtake a dawdling 70 m.p.h. milk-tanker, his arm out of the window with a V-sign on the end, but nevertheless appeared still to be listening. Osborne continued.

'And then we go and have a look at the shed. And I always double-check they haven't reorganized it since the photographer came, because otherwise I might say in the piece that it's a really neat and tidy shed and the picture shows it as a terrible mess, which makes me look stupid.'

'Right.'

'I mean, it's bad enough when I describe them wearing gumboots, and the picture shows them in sandals.'

'Right.'

'I let them know that I'm familiar with their work, because that makes them relax.'

'Right.'

'And sometimes I take flowers, if it's a woman.'

'Right.'

Makepeace was thoughtful. Osborne had evidently failed to say what he wanted to hear. 'But what about the excitement? Isn't it a buzz meeting famous people all the time?'

Osborne thought about it, but the question meant nothing to him at all. He shrugged.

'Haven't you done any interviews yourself?'

'Never.'

'Is that why you wanted to come?'

'Partly.'

'But it's not like really *meeting* these famous people, you know. I mean, you might bump into them in the street the next day and they wouldn't know you.'

'So what?'

'I mean, take this Angela Farmer. I'm positive, *positive*, I have met her before, but I know for an absolute fact that she won't remember me.'

'You have met her, though; that's something.'

'Well, there's the difference between us. I really don't think that it is.'

Osborne was wrong, though, if he thought he had no impact on people in general, because there was one group of his acquaintance on whom he made an impression disproportionately large: women. Unlikely as it may seem, women regularly took a fancy to Osborne, against all the negative probability that a down-at-heel hack with only a few kilos of peanut brittle to his name would make a woman remotely happy in the long term. There was just something about him; something that the little squit Makepeace, for example, would never possess despite all his youth and cleverness, despite even his ginger ponytail. Even Osborne's virginal vagueness about sex, which he always modestly supposed would disqualify him from the field, paradoxically served only to fuel the attraction.

Of course, cynics might say that the phenomenon owed more to the shocking self-esteem of the women concerned than to the innate attractiveness of the man; but this insight, while undoubtedly helpful, could not account for everything. Osborne had many genuine features to commend him: a pleasant manner, decent dental hygiene, and a liberality with cup cakes bordering on saintliness. To cap it all, there was an old-fashioned streak of gallantry he had somehow never shaken off – which meant that he sometimes complimented women on their appearance, opened doors for them, even kissed the backs of their hands. This knocked them dead. Such demonstrations being like showers of spring rain in the veritable Death Valley of most modern women's emotional lives, Osborne absent-mindedly picked up female admirers the way other people pick up fluff.

Michelle, of course, had fancied him for twelve years, a fact that anyone but Osborne would have deduced long ago from her wildly divergent behaviour towards him. Why else would someone appear to be so cloyingly sweet one minute, and the next as punchy as a boxing kangaroo? It is a sure sign of thwarted passion in a naturally forceful person such as Michelle. But Osborne, unable to penetrate the mystery, merely assumed that when she was nice, she was attempting to give him the benefit of the doubt; and when she was nasty, it was because, understandably, she found she couldn't, after all.

Those spoof letters she wrote to Osborne from the unfortunate red-herring address in Honiton were only the latest of dozens she had written for her own amusement and then filed carefully in a special place in the office. In each brace of letters, moreover, she had conformed to the same schizoid pattern, making it a rule that for each saucy epistle there would be a reproving one of equal strength. Looking back on the two letters that (thanks to Lillian) had got away, she was proud of the part about the gold flip-flops and the gardening gloves, but relieved, on the whole, not to have made reference on this occasion to a particular sexual fantasy that recurred in the letters as it recurred in her dreams. She didn't want to scare anyone unnecessarily, even under a false name. But this fantasy, for what it is worth, entailed the tying of Osborne's wrists with garden twine, the staking of his body to a freshly turned flower-bed, and the stroking of his exposed nipples, ever so lightly, with the sharpened tines of a rusty, jumbo pitchfork. In some obscure way which Michelle had never dared pause to analyse, the idea gave her enormous pleasure.

Approaching Stonehenge, Makepeace ventured, 'Perhaps you know Angela Farmer in the biblical sense.' Osborne took a moment to guess what his friend might be getting at, because his mind immediately leapt to Angela Farmer as the redoubtable Eve in *Forgive Us Our Trespasses* – in which case, of course, he *did* know her in the biblical sense, as did millions and millions of other people.

'Are you talking about sex, Makepeace? Are you suggesting *Angela Farmer* would have sex with me? The well-known glamorous person? You must be further off your trolley than I thought.'

'Why not? You're a nice-looking bloke. I've seen how the women look at you down at the Birthplace of Aphrodite.'

Osborne suddenly felt rather warm and unbuttoned his coat. His window steamed up.

'Just drop it,' he said.

'You'd make a nice couple, you and Angela – and the tulip. And she must have *buckets* of money.'

'Look –'

'You should get in there, I'm not joking. Take her some flowers. Tell her she's got the nicest shed you've ever seen. Something like that.'

'Leave it, please.'

'I'll bet you two dozen cup cakes she remembers you.'

'Shut up. I mean it.'

It was just getting dark when they finally located their boarding house. Fortunately there were unlikely to be two B&Bs with a name like Dunquenchin in a small town like Honiton. 'What does it mean, for fuck's sake – that they've given up alcohol?' asked Makepeace, as he noisily wrestled the bike out of the back of the van on Dunquenchin's gravel drive. 'Big fucking deal.' He had been a bit tetchy ever since the conversation about Ms Farmer, Osborne had noticed, and was starting to behave in the manner of a loose cannon. Perhaps Osborne's notorious helplessness with street-maps had annoyed him (it annoyed most people); perhaps something nasty once happened to him in a town famous for lace and traffic jams. Either way, he had started to say 'Fuck' a lot, so it was fair to assume that something was up. 'Fuck!' he now exclaimed for no apparent reason, as he fixed the bits of his bike together. 'Oh, fuck *this!*'

'You all right?' asked Osborne.

'Fuck off.'

'We made it, though.'

'Dun-fuckin-quenchin,' Makepeace went on. 'Jesus Fuck, what the fuck is that?'

Osborne wondered momentarily whether he had somehow stumbled into a Martin Scorsese movie, but he looked around and he was definitely still in Honiton at lighting-up time.

'I expect there's an explanation,' he said in an attempt to mollify.

'An explanation, he says. Fucking great. Mister Oz reckons there's an explanation. So what will you be calling *your* retirement cottage, Mister Oz? Dun-buggerin-about? Or just Dun-doin-fuck-all?'

Osborne tried to ignore this, merely dragging his bag to the front door and peering in the dark for the doorbell. This was scarcely the right time to fall out with Makepeace, because for one thing they had booked a double room. He found the doorbell and pressed it. 'Better than Dun-bloody-knowing-it-all,' he muttered, but loudly enough for Makepeace to hear. Which was probably a mistake.

Makepeace threw the bike down with a clatter (that ominous *tring!*) and strode towards him, almost at a run.

'Dun *what?*' he bellowed. Good grief, it was the horror of the pomegranates all over again. Osborne stifled a scream. 'Dun *fucking what?*'

At which point, luckily, the door opened to reveal the rather dramatic silhouette of a large man in an old fireman's jacket, and Makepeace skidded to a halt on the stones. Osborne looked around in amazement. The man, who was observing Makepeace coolly from the step, appeared to be holding a metal hatchet in his hand, possibly with the intention of using it. Everything went terribly quiet. 'It's called Dunquenchin,' he said softly to Osborne, absently polishing the blade with a large white hanky. 'Does your friend' – here he pointed with the weapon – 'have a problem with that?'

'Oh no, I don't think so,' said Osborne.

'Mm.'

'I'm really sorry about the shouting,' continued Osborne, 'but he's been driving all day, and he's a bit wound up.'

'Wound up?' said the man. 'As Jeff Bridges so wittily remarks in *The Fabulous Baker Boys*, he's a bloody alarm clock.' They looked together at Makepeace, who had gone back to the van and was now inexplicably stamping on the ground in fury, as though involved in a strange Cossack dance of his own devising.

'He'll be all right if he can have a drink, I expect. "Dunquenchin" doesn't mean you don't serve drink, I hope?'

'No, only that I don't put out fires.'

Osborne looked at the uniform and said, 'Ah.'

'Just been giving a talk to some lacemakers. They loved the hatchet.'

'I see.'

'You on business?'

'Oh yes.'

'Name?'

'We booked under the name of Makepeace. That's him.'

The fireman considered him for a moment.

'What does your friend do, apart from impressions of Rumpelstiltskin?'

'He's a writer.'

'You don't say. What does he write?'

'Book reviews, mostly.'

'It takes all sorts.'

Nobody else was staying at Dunquenchin that night, which was not surprising given the season. In the evening, therefore, Osborne and Makepeace sat alone in the small, chilly dining-room consuming a fairly good home-made soup, cream of cauliflower, and staring in glum silence at their host's many fire-service mementoes decking the walls. Normal talk was impossible: for a start, Makepeace had overheard the Rumpelstiltskin comparison and was still sulking; but on top of that they both laboured under the usual inhibition of self-conscious visitors to guesthouses, a paranoid conviction that their conversation, however banal, was being not only overheard but possibly also written down.

Nothing could be further from the truth, of course, since the fireman obeyed the corollary rule of guesthouses, which says that the host pays very little attention to the diners ('Brr, are you sure you're warm enough?' he said, not waiting for an answer, as he whisked away the soup bowls), and that the meal must be prepared with the maximum rumpus and no self-consciousness whatever about kitchen conversation travelling straight to the ears of the guests. So, 'I gave them the last of the cauliflower soup,' they heard him say to someone on the other side of the thin swing door. They tried not to listen, but they couldn't help it. 'Oh,' replied another, younger, male voice. 'Hadn't it gone a bit whiffy?' Osborne scratched his nose and looked hard at a shiny helmet, a medal and a large full-colour photo of a warehouse conflagration in 1975 – presumably a fire with happy memories for his host. 'What are they getting next, then?' the conversation continued. 'One of my famous risottos.' 'Blimey, Dad, is that all? You're not exactly pushing the boat out.' 'Well, they're a bit obnoxious, if you must know.' 'Oh, I see. How many nights?' 'Just the one, I hope.' 'Good.'

'Shall we go out for a drink after this?' asked Makepeace in a low whisper.

'Good idea.'

'I was in a bit of a mood earlier on.'

'I noticed.'

'I get moods like that sometimes.'

'Right.' If this was Makepeace's way of saying sorry, 'Right' was all he was getting in return.

'I don't like it here.'

'Nor do I.'

There was a pause.

'Did you think the soup was whiffy?' asked Osborne.

Makepeace didn't reply.

There was another long pause while they stared at the walls, and the word 'obnoxious' bounced around the room.

Suddenly Makepeace let out a little shriek. 'Oh, fucking hell,' he rasped. 'Look. You see the name on all this fireman crap? It's Clarke.'

Osborne looked puzzled. 'Clarke? What do you mean?'

'Look at it,' hissed Makepeace. '*Clarke. Of Honiton.* You know. The flip-flops. It could be *him*, our friend with the shiny buttons.'

'Oh, for heaven's sake!' exclaimed Osborne, forgetting to keep his voice down.

Makepeace signalled at him furiously, so he shut up. But Osborne was confused. Was this a joke, or what?

'Listen.' Makepeace now sounded urgent. He had picked up a spoon and was studying it carefully, as though thinking his way out of a dangerous situation. 'Think back,' he hissed, importantly. 'Does he know who you are? Did you give your name or anything when you booked?'

Osborne thought about it. 'No, I gave yours. But –'

'Whatever you do, don't tell him, then. Funny letters are one thing, but he's got a hatchet. Next thing you know, you'll be on a one-way journey to the shed in a fireman's lift.'

'Listen, this is stupid.' Osborne started to get up from the table, but at this point the door burst open and a young man with carroty hair entered with two bowls of steaming dinner, a side salad and a basket of bread, most of it precariously balanced on his forearms. He plonked it down, gave them a pleasant non-committal sort of smile, said, 'Hello I'm Gordon, hope you're warm enough in here, not very warm though is it,' and promptly disappeared again, to rejoin the conversation off-stage.

Gordon. They looked at one another. That made him G. Clarke.

'It's him, then!' said Makepeace. 'The boy! It's him!'

But by now Osborne had had enough. 'All right, shut up,' he said. 'This is bloody silly. Just because his dad said you looked like Rumpelstiltskin, there's no need –'

'Come and "rummage in my shed", big boy,' Makepeace continued. "Phew, hot work, gardening".'

'I'm not listening.'

'Keep your voice down,' commanded Makepeace, and jerked his head towards the door so vehemently that they stopped arguing and started listening again. Which was unfortunate, really, the way things turned out later on.

'Have you sent those *Come Into the Garden* letters yet, Gordon?' shouted the older man over the drumming of water in a washing-up bowl.

'Not yet,' his son yelled back.

'You ought to do it soon. I mean, if it's urgent.'

'I know.'

Osborne gulped. Makepeace, astounded, burst out laughing. 'Urgent!' he repeated, and pointed at Osborne's face.

'You know I don't like to interfere,' Gordon's dad continued. 'But I just wonder whether you've got mixed feelings. You could ease up, you know.'

'Ha!' exclaimed Makepeace in triumph. 'Mixed feelings!' And he slapped his thigh.

'Listen, Dad,' said Gordon, 'I know what I'm doing. I know when I'm out of my depth. Trust me. You remember how you worried about *Digger*?'

'I know.'

'I can handle it.'

'All right.'

'I'll see to the plates.'

Gordon kicked the swing door and marched into the dining-room, the fixed B&B smile already planted on his face. But what he found was that the dinner on the plates was hardly tasted, let alone finished.

'That's funny,' he shouted back to his dad. 'They've gone.'

6

Angela Farmer put down the detective novel she was reading, breathed a large blue plume of smoke and consulted her watch. Eleven fifteen. Jeeze. She would definitely have to get dressed soon. Or at least visit the bathroom. Something. For now, however, she stubbed out her cigarette in one of the ashtrays resting on her upper chest and fractionally shifted her position in the bed – just enough to feel the benefit, but not so much that she disturbed the rabbit sleeping on the eiderdown, or toppled to the floor any of the books, papers or cake boxes that seemed somehow to have piled up in heaps. Idly she thought of all the people who were currently doing healthy outdoor up-and-at-'em things, such as weeding and golf, and gave a loud, barking laugh, something along the lines of 'Arf, arf'.

Woman's Hour played at her elbow on a large portable radio. In a moment, Jenni Murray would announce, 'And now, Angela Farmer reads the second instalment of –' but the prospect gave her little satisfaction. She picked up the book again and studied the cover. It was Trent Carmichael's new title, *Murder, Shear Murder* (the latest in Michelle's favourite death-by-garden-implement series, which included *Let Them Eat Rake* and the bestselling *Dead for a Bucket*), but she put it down again.

Trent Carmichael had been a buddy ever since she starred in the TV movie of *S is for ... Secateurs!*, and he always sent her a complimentary copy of each new book, with a friendly inscription. But that didn't mean she had to *like* his goddam fiction. 'Ah,' she sighed, 'fuck him if he can't take a joke'.

'Ya OK down there – *bunny?*' she barked.

The rabbit made no move.

'Sure you don't wanna go – *walkies?*'

It didn't. Or not so as you'd notice.

Swell.

'And now,' announced Jenni Murray pointedly, 'Angela Farmer reads the second part of –'

'Oh no, she do-on't,' sang the listener gruffly, and switched herself off. Strange to feel less than contented, really. Here she was, with a new hardback, no work today, as much cake as she could eat and a faithful rabbit at her side. She could stay in bed, have a ball, sing all the songs from *Showboat*, anything. 'You could make believe I love you' (she loved doing duets); 'I could make believe that you LOVE ME.' Maybe the problem really was the book. For a third time she tried to concentrate on the deductive puzzle confronting the much-loved Inspector Greenfinger and his earthy sidekick (Pete), but for a third time failed to raise the necessary enthusiasm. 'The gardener did it,' she announced. 'My money's on the goddam gardener.' And exasperated, she threw *Murder, Shear Murder* down the bed, where it hit the bunny and woke it up.

When she had given an interview about 'a day in the life' to a Sunday magazine, by the way, it had strangely mentioned nothing of all this. Up at seven, with a healthy half-grapefruit and a few knee-bends, that's what she had told them. 'Here's my knee,' she growled, 'to prove it.' A couple of hours' light toil on the long-awaited theatrical memoirs (as yet unstarted, actually), a half-hour answering fan letters with a hunky male secretary (Gordon's dad had obligingly posed for the pictures), a low-cholesterol lunch, plus a long walk in the fresh air, and all before *The Archers* at 1.40 p.m.! It was only because her imagination ran out, and she had to invent a rather far-fetched interest in fell walking, that the interviewer ever smelled a rat.

'Oh,' he had said politely, 'fell walking. But there are no fells in Devon.'

'Sure there are. They're just so good they blend naturally into the landscape.'

'Actually, um, there aren't, you know.'

'You sure? Jesus, what a gyp.' She lit a cigarette and tried to think fast. So many daylight activity hours still to account for.

The interviewer broke the silence. 'Perhaps I could say that you do the flowers at the church, or something?'

She thought about it. 'Does that sound OK to you, not too creepy?'

'I think so.'

'Well, it's a deal. Say I do the flowers, but not every day. No one would buy that. Can you say I have a dog, too? I'd like a dog, but I never got around to getting one. And maybe an Aga where I bake cookies.'

'Fine by me, Ms Farmer. What do you want me to call it?'

'The Aga?'

'The dog.'

'Oh, yeah. Archie.'

'Nice name.'

'Thanks. I think so too.'

She could not understand actors who fretted about 'resting'. There was nothing shameful about putting your feet up; especially when, by and large, the rest of your life was hell on wheels. Yesterday she had driven to a London studio and done voice-overs all day ('The warmth of a real fire' – it was amazing how many different ways you could say it); by the weekend she had to read several lousy no-hope scripts for proposed TV sitcoms; and sometime this week she had a guy visiting from a little chicken-shit magazine to talk to her about her *outhouse*, for some cockamamy reason. So why not enjoy the peace and quiet when you had the chance?

Except that it wasn't particularly peaceful at this moment, because all of a sudden there was someone running up the stairs, and the rabbit, startled by the noise, had jumped off the bed with a thump, and was charging towards the wardrobe for cover. For Christ's sakes, what now?

'It's only me,' shouted Gordon from outside her door. 'Auntie Angela, can I come in?'

'Sure. But wait till I call off the bunny. We thought you were a burglar, and he's all riled up.'

Gordon let himself in.

'Hi,' he said, smiling.

'Hi yourself.'

'Been busy?' He waved at the chaos on the bed, the floor, the bedside table and all the available surfaces around the room. 'Good job Dad isn't here, he'd throw a fit.'

'He would.'

Gordon cleared a space carefully and sat down. 'Listen,' he said, 'I just thought I ought to warn you. There's a couple of blokes staying with us, and I heard one of them mention your name this morning. I think he's coming to see you.'

'Now why would he do that?'

'Don't know. But I think he's coming at twelve.'

Angela pursed her lips and looked at the ceiling as if to say, 'How I pity me,' but said nothing.

'Shall I check in your diary?'

'You're a doll, but I wish you wouldn't.'

'Come on, where is it?'

Angela waved a hand vaguely. 'The rabbit had it last.'

Quickly surveying the room, Gordon spotted the diary lurking in exactly the place he expected it: under a Mr Kipling Victoria Sponge. He grabbed it and riffled.

'Now, hang on ... right. Tuesday, midday. *Come Into the Garden*,' he read cheerfully, and then went terribly quiet.

Angela didn't notice the change in his demeanour. Having heaved herself out of bed, she was now kicking debris out of the way, to clear a path to the wardrobe. 'Give me *strength*,' she yelled. But at the same time as Gordon appreciatively watched her performance, laughed and started tidying things into piles, he felt oddly detached from his surroundings. *Come Into the Garden* had come to Honiton? This was dreadful. These people to whom he had just served breakfast, were they his own employees, the ones he was going to sack? No wonder they had given him odd looks. No wonder the big one looked nervous all the time, and the little one so aggressive. How they must hate him.

'How's the book?' he asked as he tidied it into a neat stack of Battenbergs and Madeiras. He needed time to think.

Angela called out from inside her walk-in wardrobe.

'Borrow it if you like. But it's gruesome, I warn you now. These two misfit guys turn up at a house in the country, behave in such a weird manner that they attract lots of attention, and then a young red-headed nineteen-year-old squire is found dead, stabbed fatally with a pair of shears.'

Gordon looked thoughtful.

'What's the motive?' he asked tentatively.

'Some grudge.'

'Oh.'

'It's kinda hazy.'

'But did they do it?'

'Good question. I figure the gardener. It's usually the disgruntled employee, in my experience.'

'Oh.'

'I think the trouble is he writes too much. Trent Carmichael, I mean. He's a kind of production line. When he rang me Saturday, he told me he'd already half-finished the next one – I don't know, *Dead-head Among the Roses*, or some such miserable thing. Oh, but he told me something interesting. He'd had the same guy around to interview him about his goddam shed. I mean, your pal from Dunquenchin.'

'What?'

'Said it was strange, though. The guy never asked any of the obvious questions – about the shears and rakes in the stories. Trent figured he was either very deep or very stupid, so he rang up and asked for a copy of the piece. But when they faxed it to him, he said it was amazing: the guy must have been a huge fan, with a real taste for this stuff. He catalogued all the murders, including even the shears in this one, and the book's only been out a week. He'd done some big heavy-duty homework. Trent was very impressed. Said the guy had a real understanding of the mad, vengeful, homicidal mind.'

Gordon broke a Victoria Sponge in half, stared at the cream and jam, and felt suddenly very lonely and small. He wanted his daddy. He couldn't stop thinking about how he had just served breakfast to two men who quite conceivably wished to kill him. It was silly, obviously. People didn't go around killing people, not because a little magazine folded. Get serious. But on the other hand, something was definitely going on with these guys. Why else, at breakfast, had the big one visibly flinched when Gordon touched his hand by mistake as he put down the toast rack? 'Aagh!' he had cried. 'Lay off with that!' the other one had shouted, jumping to his feet. They were edgy all right. It all made horrible sense.

Dad must be told at once. Gordon had left him on his own in the house with them. There was just one little problem with Gordon's theory: how on earth could these men *know* about Digger Enterprises' plans for the magazine? Surely nobody knew, besides Dad (who was currently faxing an official letter to the editor of *Come Into the Garden*, to put everyone in the picture). But the individual letters of dismissal had only just gone in the post.

'Well, what do you think?'

Gordon looked up to see Auntie Angela stunningly attired in a bright blue pullover, smart leggings and long boots.

'Terrific.'

She kissed him. 'Thanks, Gordon, baby. Next to the rabbit, you're my favourite person.'

He smiled.

'Now, skedaddle while I put on my face, and I'll come see you later. How's that?'

'Right you are,' he said, and made for the door. But he turned back. 'Will you be all right on your own?'

'Why? Do you want to stay?'

Gordon thought about it. Auntie Angela alone in the shed with two dangerous desperadoes, and all those shears and trowels and buckets lying about. 'Actually, it might be an idea,' he said.

'Fine, if you want to. Listen, you can double for me at the interview too, if you like. Put on a frock or something. This nightie would suit you – catch. You know more about that goddam shed than I do, that's for sure.'

Back at the offices of *Come Into the Garden*, a fax was coming through. Since Lillian kept the machine beside her desk, between the standard lamp and the magazine rack (in front of the framed reproduction of *The Haywain*), she was in a position to turn it off most of the time; but today, by some stroke of misfortune, she had forgotten. She hated the disruption to her concentration (she was knitting a cable stitch in fluorescent orange – she always wore bright colours), but since she was frightened to turn it off once it had started operating, she now merely glared at the missive as it slowly and noisily emerged, bottom first, and tried to imagine what life was like before the invention of telecommunication. 'Honiton, Devon', it said; then, after a bit of high-pitched whirring, 'G. Clarke'. This was going to take for ever. 'Yours sincerely'. Lillian fretted impatiently, but then saw the final line of the letter: 'I am sorry to bring you and your staff such bad news.'

Death knells don't only come in bongs, then. This one didn't go bong, or ding, or clang, even faintly. It just made a nasty insistent electronic noise, in the manner of faxes everywhere, and a grave two-minute silence would have been distinctly out of place. Looking around, in fact, it was plain to see that office life was proceeding with quite ghastly normality. Tim – attempting to make a cup of tea – sniffed some milk in an open carton and recoiled so violently that he hit his head on a pillar and his glasses fell off. Next door, Michelle spoke to the typesetters by phone, asking them with a deadly sweetness, far be it from her, etcetera, whether it would be too much trouble for them to 'set some type', perhaps in the spirit of experiment, to find out whether they could take to it, given time and the right circumstances. And a motorcycle messenger, despairing of ever gaining Lillian's attention, slowly surrendered to narcolepsy on a chair, his heavy, shiny, helmeted head coming finally to rest on his leather-clad knees, giving him the appearance of a black coiled-up bean-sprout.

All this blithe normality! How incredibly ironic! When just a few yards away fate was unfolding, slowly and backwards, with only Lillian to know.

She tore the message off the machine and read it through, several times. She even read it bottom-up a few times, too, just to recapture the original sensation of receiving it. And then she put it in her top drawer and turned the lock. She peered at the motorcycle messenger and decided it would be a shame to wake him.

'Not from the elusive Mr Makepeace, I suppose?'

Michelle was passing, on her way to the sandwich shop, and had spotted the fax.

'No,' snapped Lillian, 'it wasn't.'

'Lackaday,' said Michelle, not as a joke. 'Could I ask you to be preternaturally sweet and keep an eye peeled for his book round-up?'

Lillian gave her a look that said No, actually, Michelle could not ask her to be as sweet as all that. In fact, just try it. And as for the peeled eye, what an unpleasant turn of phrase.

'You see, between these four walls, Lillian – these four quaint but cosy living-room walls, I suppose I should say,' she added, glancing at Lillian's magazine rack, 'I suspect Mr Makepeace of making things up. He keeps missing deadlines, but instead of apologizing he says, "Didn't you get it? I posted it on Friday." I asked Osborne to tell him we haven't received the latest piece, and I just *know* he's going to pretend he's done it already.'

'Huh,' said Lillian.

'Well, it's annoying!' exclaimed Michelle, suddenly quite heated. 'It's unprofessional. When he says, "I posted it on Friday," I have to pretend I believe him, because I can't accuse him of lying. I hate it. And I don't understand why Osborne has befriended him, either. What can he see in a jerk like Makepeace, who can't stop telling lies?'

In fifteen years, Lillian had rarely heard such passion from Michelle. It was rather entertaining. Did she say 'jerk'?

'Want me to sort him out?' said Lillian flatly.

'I don't understand.'

'I could sort him out. I'm good at sorting out liars.' Herewith, she tapped her locked drawer significantly, and gave Michelle a level stare.

'You've lost me, I'm afraid,' said Michelle. She shoved the swing door and marched out, leaving Lillian to her own devices.

'Oh yes,' said Lillian to herself, 'I'm very good with liars.'

'I'm going back,' said Makepeace. They had reached Angela Farmer's gate; and Osborne was stooping to pick up the nice bunch of flowers he had dropped, nervously, for the second time; and hoping he wouldn't topple over, through sheer nerves, when he tried to regain the upright position. The long walk to the front door always took him this way; he reckoned it was the adrenalin. Fight or flight, they called it. Which was fair enough, since he would certainly have fought anyone who tried to stop him running away.

'What?' he said. 'Going back? You mean you aren't coming in?'

'No, I'm not.'

Osborne was confused. 'But I thought you wanted to meet her.'

'I never said that.'

'You did.'

'I fucking didn't.'

'Oh. Mm. Right.'

The older man needed a minute to take this in. 'Oh well,' he said, trying to sound regretful, 'I suppose if you're going back now, I can always catch a train. Tsk, don't worry, I can manage. After all, it's up to you, it's your car –'

'No,' interrupted his friend. 'I mean, I'm going back to Dunquenchin.'

Osborne looked at him. He had made his announcement as though 'going back to Dunquenchin' was something that a man's gotta do.

'But they've both gone out. The boy went out first, and then the fireman. Don't you remember, we saw him from the florist's? I waved, and he pretended not to see us. In any case, what's the fascination? If that boy is a bit funny about me, isn't it better just to get away and forget about it? He didn't know who I was, so no harm done.'

'But I want to find out who Digger was.'

'Digger?'

'Last night, he said his dad shouldn't have worried about Digger, because everything had been under control. Perhaps he felt about Digger the way he feels about you.'

'Stop it, mate. It's not worth it. Let's just do the interview and go home.'

'No.'

'Have a cup cake?'

'Fucking *no!*'

'How will you get in, in any case?'

'I unlocked the back door this morning, when I was taking my bike out.'

'I don't like it.'

'You don't have to. You just be nice to Ms Farmer and sit in her shed, and I'll do the rest.'

It would be fair to say that when Gordon opened the door at Ms Farmer's, holding a pale blue négligé in his hand, Osborne did not rise above his emotions.

'Aagh!' he exclaimed, and dropped the flowers again.

'Didn't expect to see me?' said Gordon carefully. This is the only way to deal with these people, he decided. Don't let them see you are afraid.

'Well, not so soon,' admitted Osborne jumpily. 'Er, I've got some – well, business with Ms Farmer, if that's all right.' Don't say what it is, thought Osborne. For God's sake, don't tell him you are the shed man at *Come Into the Garden*.

They looked at one another. There was a long pause.

'I know,' said Gordon.

They both took a deep breath.

'I know who you are. And I think I know why you've come. You're from *Come Into the Garden*, aren't you? You're the man who does the sheds.'

Oh God. Osborne gulped. ''Assright,' he said in a tiny voice.

'I know your work,' said Gordon very carefully.

'Oh good. Er, thank you very much.'

'Where's your friend?'

Osborne started guiltily. 'Nowhere,' he said. 'I mean, I don't know. Nothing to do with me, anyway.'

'You'd better come in,' said Gordon.

'No, it's all right,' said Osborne with a brave smile. 'I'm fine here.'

'I think you should.'

'No, it's a lovely day. Tell you what, where's the shed? I'll start there.'

Back at Dunquenchin, Makepeace had climbed the stairs to Gordon's modest little office – a top-storey room with a tiny window, and very little sign of Gordon's immense success. It was nearer to an average teenager's playroom than to an executive office, with papers and gadgets and bits of computer scattered about like toys. What it did have, however, was a fax machine, something Makepeace spotted at once. Could this be his perfect opportunity to clear himself with *Come Into the Garden*? If not, why not? Despite the rather stressful circumstances, this was too good a chance to miss. Hastily he scribbled a note to *Come Into the Garden*, and fed it, without more ado, into the fax.

Dear Michelle,

Hi! Osborne tells me you didn't get my round-up last Friday. Are you absolutely sure? Because I came to the office specially and posted it in your letter-box on Thursday night. It was two sides of A4, green typewriter-ribbon. I can't imagine what could have happened to it. Anyway, I can type it up again by Friday if you like. What a drag!

In haste (in Devon!),
M. Makepeace

'Why didn't he come in?' asked Angela. 'I don't get it.'

Gordon considered. 'I just think he's a bit peculiar.'

'Well, I'll drink to that. Shall I go out and speak to him, do you think? I mean, if he's just gonna look at the shed on his own, I needn't have got up so early. I mean, now I think of it, I needn't have got up at all.'

They were watching from the kitchen window.

'Listen, can I phone Dad? It's just that the other one, his pal, isn't with him, and I'm a bit worried what he might be up to.'

'Gordon, this isn't like you, sweetheart. What's on your mind?'

'Well, it may just be rubbish, but I think these blokes might be a bit desperate. I don't know; out for revenge, or something like that.'

'I get it. Your dad did one of his risottos, am I right?'

'No. I mean, yes. But that's not it. Can I use the phone?'

'Sure.'

'Thanks.'

'Don't mention it.'

Makepeace was startled when the phone rang, and even more alarmed when he heard it answered downstairs. 'Fuck,' he said aloud, and then wished he hadn't.

'Dunquenchin,' said Gordon's dad, as though it were quite a normal thing to say, but then his tone changed. 'What on earth's the matter?' he said. 'Yeah, but I only just got in. Listen, if there's trouble I'll sort it out. You stay with Angela, and I'll be with you as soon as I can.'

Just then the fax machine started to rumble, and Makepeace panicked. Gordon's dad was looking for him! The big man with the beach-ball shoulders and those searing Rumpelstiltskin analogies! Oh God. Should he hide, jump out of the window, what? Why hadn't he picked up a hatchet from downstairs, or a ladder, or a large colour picture to hide behind? And now this sodding machine was giving him away. 'Shut up!' he hissed at it, and rushed over to turn it off. But glancing at the message emerging from the machine, he realized to his considerable discomfort that it was addressed to him, and was a reply from *Come Into the Garden*. Oh fuck, how incriminating! Even if he hid, Gordon's dad would find out what he'd been doing. As soon as it was finished he ripped it from the machine and stared at it in horror.

> Dear Makepeace,
> Michelle wanted me to tell you not to worry about the round-up piece. She says it was on her desk all the time!

('No!' he whimpered.)

> Sorry for the false alarm! Thank goodness you haven't 'retyped' it yet, eh? She says it was pretty good, by the way, but she wasn't sure about the reference to 'hoist by his own petard' – perhaps a twinge too literary, she said.

(Makepeace struggled for breath.)

> Anyway, the point is, stop worrying! You writers are all far too conscientious!
>
> All best,
> Lillian

'Fuck!' shouted Makepeace. The effect of this letter was quite extraordinary. He had started hyperventilating. In fact, he was bent double and panting when Gordon's dad put his head round the door and saw him.

'Gotcha,' said the fireman softly. And standing outside, he gently but firmly turned the door-key in the lock.

7

You might suppose that Osborne Lonsdale of *Come Into the Garden* had reached the stage in his career when he could no longer be surprised by a shed. He might have thought so himself. But this would be to reckon without the *shedus mirabilis* which was now revealed to his astounded eyes in Angela Farmer's garden. How fantastic, you wonder, was Ms Farmer's shed? Well, put it this way: if Cole Porter had known anything about sheds, this amazing specimen would have featured in the famous lyric 'You're the Top' alongside the *Mona Lisa*, the Tower of Pisa and something that rhymed with 'bed'.

Osborne was speechless with excitement. Having spotted the shed from the side of the house, he fairly raced towards it, clutching his airline bag and bunch of flowers with one hand and reaching out with the other, rather in the manner of someone who has been wandering aimlessly on an almost forgotten pilgrimage for the better part of his adult life and then beholds the Holy Grail, large as life and twice as graily. All thoughts of Gordon Clarke's perverse desires were banished from his mind. This shed had a chimney! It had a little garden of its own and a picket fence! It was blue! It had guttering and leaded lights!

To a man who had spent a dozen years dressing up boring

sheds for the benefit of his readers, Angela Farmer's exceptional shed was like manna from heaven; his heart filled with praise. Forget the Cole Porter thing and put it this way instead: if the *Magnificat* had been about sheds, Osborne would have dropped down on his knees and sung it. For one thing, all those years devoted to looking at second-rate sheds were now utterly vindicated: they had prepared him to bear expert witness to this wondrous structure. And for another, how immensely cheering to reflect that this week's 'Me and My Shed' piece would be an absolute doddle to write.

Angela watched him from the kitchen window, a cup of coffee in her hand.

'That man is nuts,' she said.

'Mmm,' agreed Gordon.

'He's acting like a goddam lunatic.'

'Well, I –'

'Is the bunny safely indoors? I don't want that rabbit spooked by a nutsy newspaperman.'

'It's upstairs, I think.'

'Good.'

'Actually, it was nibbling some TV script or other, the last time I saw it. I hope that was all right?'

'Sure. Why not? A rabbit needs all the roughage it can get.' She put on a coat. 'Well, I suppose I'd better go talk to the crazy-man. Don't look so worried, baby. Take my word for it, the guy is harmless. On the other hand, he does seem to be *worshipping* the outhouse. Do you suppose that's normal?'

'We had some really nice times in that shed, Auntie Angela,' said Gordon wistfully, as if nice times were emphatically a thing of the past. 'Do you remember? How you used to sing me songs?'

'I remember that you sang them too.'

'Did I?'

'Sure. Duets. "You say neither and I say nie-ther".'

Smiling, Gordon suddenly sang out, '"But oh, if we call the whole thing off, then we must part –"'

She joined in. '"But oh,"' they sang together, '"if we had to part, then that might break my heart."'

Osborne opened the little picket gate and stood enraptured. Neat little descriptive phrases were leaping in his writer's mind like salmon in the spawning season; he felt refreshed, vigorous, inspired and glad, nay proud to be the author of 'Me and My Shed'. For some reason, however, he also kept getting intrusive little flashes from a recent memory of the *Come Into the Garden* office, but he couldn't think why. He looked at his shoe – at the Tipp-Ex mark, actually – but it wasn't that. It was something to do with Tim. That's right. Tim crouching beside his desk, asking questions about Angela Farmer. All those details about sheds, about her husbands and gerbils, and umpteen sitcoms. Osborne couldn't remember much of it now, which was a nuisance.

'Barney proposed to me in that shed,' Angela told Gordon, as if reading Osborne's mind. 'You didn't know that, did you?'

'I did, I think. But I'd forgotten.'

'Well, why should you remember? He left before you and your dad moved down here; he's hardly been near me in ten years. He wasn't a man for keeping in touch.'

'Was it terrible, breaking up?'

'No, it was predictable. It was never going to work. I said "neither" and he said "nie-ther".' She grimaced. 'But to be honest, that was bearable. No, the trouble was that neither of us said "pot-ah-to". We had to call the whole thing off.'

They looked out at the big, autumnal garden, and both shivered. Gordon rarely heard a word about Barney. The ex-husband could be buried out there in the cold ground with the invisible bulbs and tubers for all the difference it would make. All Gordon knew was that Angela's second (and last) marriage had endured for just five years, and that there had been no children, even though it had been Angela's last chance of motherhood. She gave up quite a few things for that man. Before Barney, she had split her career between London and New York, but because Barney worked in British television (cockney character parts, mostly), she settled with him in England, bought the big house in Devon and the flat in town, even agreed with his decision not to have babies. And then he dumped her – just when her biological clock wound down and stopped. She never forgave him for that, and especially not for starting a family straight away with his next wife, his bimbo co-star on *For Ever and Ever Amen*. That was a real poke in the eye.

Barney was a louse, as Angela was fond of saying. He was, she said, 'of the louse, lousy'. When the Angela Farmer tulip was announced, he sent her a postcard, from completely out of the blue, saying, 'There you are, love! You got propagated after all! Ain't nature wonderful?' which made Angela so mad she set fire to the curtains.

Since Barney, there had been very few liaisons of the romantic variety, either in the shed or out of it. Angela spent most of her fifth decade alone, partly because she was happier that way, but also because the available talent for women her age was so sparse it was laughable. The brightest spot of the past ten years had occurred in a darkened cinema, when Angela saw to her amazement, in the movie *In Bed with Madonna*, that she was not the only famous glamorous woman who had trouble finding a mate. Men were intimidated by her, for God's sake. If not by her intelligence, then by her fame; if not by her independence, then by her money. Her best girlfriend in the biz, Jerry Moffat, would sometimes talk to her about all this when they met at a London hotel for cocktails, but they didn't particularly see eye to eye on the subject.

'Poor babies,' Jerry would sympathize, while a waiter

hovered nearby. 'No wonder they're threatened. They're just so insecure, don't you see?'

'Fuck that,' said Angela, handing back the bowl for more nuts. 'Let's have another drink.'

Jerry was the one friend of Angela's who did not actively hate her for her success. As Angela had warned Gordon all those years ago in the shed, when *Digger* looked set to make him famous, it is easier for a camel to thread a needle with its eye than for a friend to forgive you for being recognized in Sainsbury's on a Saturday afternoon. Even Jerry, to be honest, sometimes went home cursing after their meetings, because Angela was recognized by somebody and she wasn't. Years ago, they had made a special trip along Shaftesbury Avenue to see Angela's name being hung in lights outside a theatre. It had been Jerry's idea to do it. But then, when they got closer and saw it, and Angela said, 'Wow, can you believe that?' Jerry mysteriously jumped in a taxi and drove off, holding a large white hanky to her face.

Angela knew she didn't deserve the pariah treatment, but at least she understood the dynamic. The point was that she was funny. She was funny on stage, funny on TV, even faintly amusing in real life. Therefore the public didn't just point at her across supermarkets, they responded to her personally. They came over, smiling, with their hands outstretched. Naturally this warmed her heart, but it was extremely galling for her friends. Going around with Angela was like being the sidekick of the Most Popular Girl in the Fifth. It was enough to drive anyone back to the camels and their frustrated attempts at ocular needlepoint. Angela, to reiterate, understood this. But unfortunately she didn't see what she could do about it. And if guys were put off by it – if guys couldn't cope with the public adoring her – then they weren't worthy of the name 'guys', that's all.

'Fuck 'em,' she muttered.

'Sorry?' said Gordon.

'Forget it.'

She drained her cup and smartly zipped up her coat, the very picture of heroic resolve.

'I'm going out now,' she said. 'I may be gone for some time.'

And she struck off down the garden in the manner of Captain Oates in a blizzard, her forearm pressed against her eyes, staggering occasionally to the left. Gordon laughed. For the time being, he had entirely forgotten the existence of the *Come Into the Garden* hit-squad. There was no one in the world he liked so much as Angela.

'I want to show you something.' Lillian breezed into Tim's office and shut the door with a slam.

Tim pressed himself deep into his chair and held his breath. He really hated it when people shut the door of his room with him inside it. It made him want to scream. His glasses went all bleary with the heat rising off his jumper.

'Actually, I've got rather a lot of work just now. This feature about mulching is the worst I've ever read and Makepeace has let us down again and if I don't completely rewrite this in time for the two o'clock bike, which always comes at one forty-five I might add, it won't be set up by tomorrow and then we won't –'

Lillian snatched it from his hand and threw it in the bin.

'Oh look, your desk calendar is wrong,' she snarled.

'What?' Tim looked frantic.

It was Tuesday, wasn't it? Still Tuesday? Wasn't it?

'Just kidding,' she said. 'Got you going, though.'

Tim stared at her and felt his heart race. He didn't understand it. Lillian was the most irritating person he had ever known, but she was usually wheedling and awful, or whinging and awful. Now, suddenly, she was aggressive and awful, too, and he didn't think he could bear it.

'Look at these,' she said, and threw down on his desk a thick file full of photocopied letters. 'Go on,' she said. She seemed to mean business. In fact, he had the distinct impression that if he didn't look at these letters straight away, she would get behind him and push his head down on them, like a dog having its nose rubbed in widdle on the carpet.

'Er, thank you, Lillian.'

'Look at them.'

'Of course. But possibly later.'

'Now.'

'Right. Er, what are they, exactly?'

'They were written by someone on the staff. She has been writing letters to this magazine under a false name for several years, and I would never have said anything about it, except that this time she has gone too bloody far.'

Lillian's voice rose to an unearthly shriek. Tim looked at the file. It was an inch thick at least. 'Could you leave them with me?'

'No. You read them *now*.' She kicked a waste-bin with such force that it flew across the room and hit a partition wall, leaving a mark.

'Fine. I'll do that.'

'She's got a pash on Osborne, you understand.'

'A what?'

'She's obsessed with him.'

This was more than Tim could take in. He didn't know who this person was, but how could anyone be obsessed with *Osborne?*

'Are you sure?'

'Read the letters.'

She didn't move. Tim couldn't think how to shift her.

'I believe I can hear the phone ringing, Lillian.'

'Oh, for God's sake,' she said, sitting down on his spare chair and producing her orange knitting from a large bag, 'Get *real*.'

When Angela Farmer opened the shed door and barked for humorous effect, 'You! What do you think you're doing in there?' she disconcerted a very happy man. Osborne was gazing at the piles of sheet music, the collection of 78s, the wind-up gramophone, in silent ecstasy. What an amazing place. Only a cup cake could convert the experience into a transcendental one, he thought. Which meant he was in luck, actually, because providently he had bought a couple of boxes at the shops.

'Oh, Ms Farmer,' he exclaimed, spraying chocolate cake crumbs at her. 'Ms Farmer, I am so pleased to meet you. This is the best shed I've ever seen. I can't tell you, it's so marvellous, I –'

'Listen, it's a shed. Don't pop your cork.'

Osborne looked at her. God, he wished he could place her. What a stunning woman, what a *presence*.

'Right. You're right. I do apologize.' Hastily, he stuffed some silver cup-cake papers in his pocket and reached for his votive offering. 'Um, these flowers are for you.'

'Well, thanks.' She wiped the crumbs from her zipper-jacket and accepted the chrysanths with considerable grace. He smiled and shrugged. He was rather cute, she thought, in a ne'er-do-well, beaten-up, chocolate-cakey kind of way.

'So what do we do now?' she asked flatly. 'What's your angle?'

'Oh, ha ha, I don't really have one, actually. I'll just ask you about the shed, if that's all right.'

Angela gave him a frank, don't-mess-with-me look.

'Oh yeah, sure. That's what you told my friend Trent Carmichael last week. Just ask about the shed, you said. All that boring question-and-answer about the cat locked up overnight, remember? And then you write a brilliant piece with references to crime devices in his novels so way back and obscure that Trent himself had forgotten them. So come on, tell me what you want. I'm not going to give you stuff about how long I've owned a hosepipe if in the end you write about how I'm related metaphorically to the goddam Angela Farmer tulip. Which has been done before, I might add.'

'But you've got it all wrong,' objected Osborne.

'How?'

He thought quickly. He could hardly explain that all the clever stuff in his Trent Carmichael piece had been written by Michelle.

'Well, to be honest, mainly because this really and truly is the best shed I've ever seen, and I desperately want to write about it.'

'And of course you say that to all the girls.'

'No I don't.' Osborne was getting worried. His dream piece seemed to be slipping away fast. He would have burst into tears, if he hadn't suspected it might not be professional.

Angela patted his arm and smiled. 'Don't take any notice of me. Really. Nobody else does. Let's just sit down and talk about the goddam shed, if you want to, and then we can go and get a drink indoors. Deal?'

'Deal.'

'Right. Fire away.'

'Thanks.'

'Just let me say one thing.'

'What?'

'You're very sweet when you're confused.'

Indoors, Gordon was feeling better. He could see Auntie Angela sitting quietly in the shed with the interviewer, everything was calm, it was all right. He hummed into his cup of camomile tea, 'But oh, if we call the whole thing off, then we must part.' He danced his fingers along the work surface, in time with the music. How silly to get hysterical about these men from the magazine. They couldn't possibly know his plans, so why should they feel any animosity towards him? But even if they had somehow found out the whole story, surely it was pretty unusual for disgruntled employees to turn, in the first resort, to murder. Aside from anything else, it might hamper their case at ACAS.

So. The fact that the 'Me and My Shed' man was an expert on homicide (of the horticultural type, anyway) was sheer – or possibly shear – coincidence. Oh yes. Gordon kicked himself for being so hysterical, and took a sip of consoling camomile. If these guys were jumpy, obviously they were jumpy about something else. It wasn't his concern.

The phone rang. It was Dad.

'I've got him,' he said breathlessly.

'Do what, Dad?'

'I've got the little writer. You keep the big one occupied, and I'll come and take care of him, too.'

'Er, Dad,' ventured Gordon, 'when you say you've "got" him, what do you mean?'

'I've locked him in your office.'

Gordon could hardly believe his ears.

'What was he doing in there? Did you ask him in? What happened?'

'He had *broken in*, Gordon. You were right, there's something really fishy going on.'

There was a pause.

'Gordon? You all right, son?'

'What's he doing now?'

'I don't know, he's gone quiet. But I think he's tampering with your computer.'

'What a nerve.'

'Shall I come over for the other one?'

'I suppose you'd better.'

'I'll be there as quickly as I can.'

But back at Dunquenchin, Gordon's dad did pause momentarily to take a few deep breaths before swinging out of the front door with his hatchet. Blimey, he thought, it was really tough being so macho all the time. Why couldn't somebody else deal with this? Why was it that whenever he looked around in a crisis, he seemed to be the only grown-up in sight? 'Is it a bird?' they said. 'Is it a plane? No, it's Gordon's parent (male).'

Standing in the dining-room, considering whether to put down the hatchet and proceed unarmed, he felt a sudden surge of resentment. He looked at the pictures on the walls – all of them, when you came to think about it, mementoes of a career spent dousing other people's fires, extinguishing other people's cock-ups. It was part of family history that when Gordon was little, he had noticed an astrology column in a newspaper and said, 'You're Aquarius, aren't you, Dad?', to which he had replied that actually he wasn't. 'But you must be,' persisted Gordon, 'you're the water-carrier.'

Of course it was useless to argue, at this stage of life, with one's personal destiny. And if being a cross between a tower of strength and a perpetual bucket of water was his – well, at least it was better than being a poison dwarf like the little chancer locked upstairs. 'The honorary Aquarian' was how Angela described him whenever she saw him in the vicinity of water – be it running a bath, watering the garden, washing the car, or just filling the kettle for a cup of tea. She admired him very much, and liked the way the title dignified him. One day, if he was agreeable, she fancied commissioning a classical fountain for the garden modelled on Gordon's dad, with him dressed up holding a trident and bewhiskered like the source of the Thames. She visualized him surrounded by an interesting, splashy, post-modern medley of water receptacles ancient and new – deep classical urns and pitchers, of course, but mixed up with buckets and standpipes and hydrants.

Why he had given up being a fireman nobody knew, but sometimes when Angela came to dinner and they all talked late, he dropped a hint or two about a woman in London he had known; also a fire in Hammersmith, in which a friend had died. He often dreamed of fires, but didn't discuss it much, the way the heat and flames encroached on him in the night. Once he had spoken of it with his niece Margaret, because she seemed interested, but unfortunately she rather abused the confidence, and so he learned it was best to keep his own counsel. Margaret was currently studying for a master's degree in psychology at a London college, and whenever she came to stay, she affected a huge interest both in Gordon's computer stuff and in his dad's dreams. The trouble, however, was that she was extraordinarily insensitive. So the moment she acquired an insight into someone else's imagination, she used it as a blunt instrument with which to knock them down.

'You're scared of impotence, it's obvious,' she had declared to Gordon's dad, simply, between bites of dinner. 'It informs everything you do. By the way, is there any more of this? It's not very good but it fills a hole, if you know what I mean.' Another time she had called Gordon's dad on the phone quite late at night because something had struck her, and it couldn't wait until the morning. 'You should call that house "The Four Elements",' she had declared. 'You cover the whole range! Do you get it? Here's Gordon with his higher mind and his *Digger*, all air and earth; do you see? And here's you, all fire and water. Wow! No wonder you complement each other so well. Did I ever tell you about my last boyfriend? How he dug up some bulbs once when he was a child *to see if they were growing*? Can you believe that? Isn't it marvellous?' At which she snorted loudly, rather like a pig, and hung up.

Tim had always regretted telling Margaret that story. Margaret was the girlfriend who had moved out quite recently, you may remember, leaving just the cat behind. Digging up the bulbs had been silly, but that was all. It was on a par with opening the oven door to check on a soufflé: you learn from it, and then don't do it again. And that's it; it's dead and buried. Yet fate had somehow contrived to make him pay for it over and over, with Margaret shovelling loam like a madwoman, to dig up the story whenever he least wanted to hear it.

Living with Margaret, he nowadays reflected, was like being with a fanatical resurrectionist, forever exhuming for the benefit of science all the stuff he had taken special care to bury in an unmarked spot. What a relief she had gone, really. Now he could bury things for good, if he felt like it – and generally he did. These letters from G. Clarke of Honiton, for example: if Lillian hadn't known all about them already, he would gladly have paid a funeral director out of his own pocket to bury the whole lot six feet under.

'So what do you think?' asked Lillian, her eyes flashing. 'It's Michelle, you know. Michelle wrote them. She's mad. She's got to be stopped.'

Tim pulled himself together and gave her a solemn look.

'I think you should put them away,' he said, 'and forget all about them.'

It was precisely the wrong thing to say in the circumstances, because Lillian went berserk.

'But she's *crackers*, you bloody neurotic!' she yelled with great and surprising volume. 'Good bloody God! Sit there in your fancy bloody knitwear and tell me to forget about it – well, I won't! You're a weed, that's what you are! Are you saying Osborne shouldn't be warned that Michelle wants to poke his nipples with a pitchfork? Are you?'

Tim tried to interject, but somehow failed to raise a squeak.

'To think I considered knitting you a woolly!' she yelled. 'Ha! And you'd rather forget it, would you, that she's getting Makepeace to send faxes from Devon telling us that the magazine is closed! Yes, Makepeace! He's in on it, too, you know! He sent a fax from the same number within ten minutes of this bloody "G. Clarke" thing arriving. And Osborne is with him down there, for the Angela Farmer piece! And God knows what plans they've got for him between them. Forget all about it? Not bloody likely, you spotty-faced wimp!' She snatched the letters from the desk, and grabbed the door-handle. 'God, you make me puke!'

On which departing words she wrenched open his office door with such sudden energy that all the staff gathered outside to hear the shouting didn't have time to run off, and were caught standing there with their mouths open.

'Get out of my way!' she yelled, and grabbed her coat (a bright pink one). It was extraordinary. Lillian was transformed by fury. If her husband had been present, he would scarcely have recognized her. This was no poor ickle bunny, that's for sure. Or if it was, this was one little bunny that, in Angela Farmer's words, was all riled up.

8

When Osborne Lonsdale came to look back on his momentous trip to Honiton, it was the surprising moment when he was carried bodily from Angela Farmer's shed in a fireman's lift that probably stayed with him most vividly. One moment he was gazing transfixed into the actress's eyes, and feeling with a mixture of pleasure and alarm the unambiguous squeeze of her hand on his knee, and the next – well, he wasn't. The door flew open, a large human silhouette blotted the light, and then his feet left the ground and he was hanging over someone's shoulder, with all the blood rushing to his head. He was so surprised that he didn't have time to think. All that flashed through his mind was the rather curious reflection that if someone were to shove a microphone under his nose and say, 'Which would you prefer, sir: this weird upside-down thing that's happening to you now, or a chance to clean the Augean stables?' he would have opted, without hesitation, for the horse-shit.

He didn't struggle. That was the funny thing about Osborne. He was quite resigned. And as he later sat on the cold lino of the small upstairs junk-room in which he had been locked by Gordon's dad without a word of explanation, a feeble 'Bugger' was all he could muster by way of complaint. Osborne suffered, unfortunately, from a rare and debilitating conviction that when nasty things occurred in his life, he must somehow have deserved them. So instead of the more conventional 'Why me?' he tended to ask 'Why not?' Hopeless, really. Instead of 'You'll pay for this!' it was 'I expect I'm paying for something!' Arguably, then, the most distressing aspect for Osborne of being locked in a room miles from London by three crackpot strangers manifestly stronger, faster and quicker-witted than himself (and all with palpable designs on his body) was that it pointed to a past sin so heinous that it was a double disgrace not to be able to recollect it.

It was natural to be scared, however, especially if a friend (was it really Michelle?) had once lent you a copy of Stephen King's thriller *Misery*, with all the most gruesome torture bits marked so deeply with a sharp pencil that there were actually holes in the paper. Osborne had started reading *Misery* comfortably one evening in his safe south London billet at about half-past eight, pouring himself a small brandy and listening to records; and finished it wide-eyed, stark sober, hyperventilating and peeing himself at four o'clock the following morning to the scary early-hours amplified hum of electric lights. For reasons obvious to anyone familiar with this book's memorable plot, aspects of it now jumped up and down in Osborne's imagination, shrieking. In *Misery*, a hapless writer is held captive by his 'Number One Fan' and made to write pulp fiction, under duress! Meanwhile, the fan indicates to him in various unignorable ways that she is dangerously off her rocker! She gets him addicted to drugs! Cuts his foot off! With an axe! Was this what fate had in store for Osborne, our inoffensive shed-man? Would Mad Gordon appear in flip-flops and négligé at any moment with a hatchet, a typewriter and a fistful of amphetamines?

Anyone else might have screamed at this point. But Osborne was not everyone. Rearranging himself more comfortably on the floor, and taking a few deep breaths, he attempted, believe it or not, to look on the bright side. You had to hand it to him – really. Say the worst happened, he reasoned. Well, he had been meaning to write a novel for ages; this could be his big chance. Oh yes. As for the drugs thing, well, for heaven's sake, why *not* try drugs? Especially in a controlled environment, and especially (he added as a plucky afterthought) if he wasn't going anywhere, *having only the one foot*. Something about that foot amputation failed to present itself in any cheery aspect, despite efforts. But otherwise it was a brave try, and for a while it completely took his mind off the other, more pressing, thing that most people would have been doing in the circumstances, i.e. plotting their escape.

Bugger. He suddenly leapt to his feet. Should he be tying sheets together, or something? Fashioning a crude weapon from a razor-sharp sliver of window pane and a ripped-off table leg? Starting a small fire and banging on the door? Well, probably, yes. For a few moments, Osborne stood rooted to the spot, but gesturing wildly in different directions as though intending to sprint off somewhere when he'd made up his mind. But the access of energy did not last, and he soon sat down again, defeated before he'd begun. Funny how the survival instinct did not apply to everyone, he reflected. When they were giving it out, he must have been too scared to step forward.

Once, he had discussed this matter with Makepeace down at the Birthplace of Aphrodite, mentioning as a case in point the remarkable behaviour of passengers in air disasters. If there is a fire at the back of a plane, he told Makepeace with astonishment, these people just climb over each other, every man for himself; then they jam the doorways and die. 'I know,' said Makepeace, 'so what?' 'Well, I just don't think I'd do that,' he had replied, baffled. 'Yes you would,' said Makepeace flatly, 'because everyone would.' Osborne looked at him and shook his head. 'But can you imagine yourself doing it?' he persisted. 'Of course,' replied Makepeace with a tinge of exasperation. And he meant it. Afterwards Osborne found it hard to shake off the mental image of Makepeace on an aircraft blithely clambering over upturned faces not for any reason of life or death, but just to get first crack at the loos.

It was at least half an hour before he noticed the rabbit. When at last he registered its presence, it was chewing a photograph album; and to judge from the shreds of assorted paper and cloth on the carpet, this item was only the entrée in a many-coursed banquet now in full swing. Osborne also noticed that an electric flex for a small bar-fire had been gnawed right through. Oh great. An electrical fire was probably the last thing he needed (if you didn't count the fairly unlikely sudden appearance on his ankle of a dotted line marked 'Cut Here with Axe'). Osborne remembered with a shudder how one of his house-sitting experiences had been quite ruined by a pet rabbit chewing through the cable to the washing machine and causing a small explosion. A flash and a bang from the utility room had been followed by the sight of a rather dazed bunny with all its fur sticking out hopping lopsidedly into the living-room and then falling over. The rabbit was never the same again. If you held up three fingers and said 'How many?' it just looked at you.

Watching this rabbit of Angela Farmer's, however, Osborne felt strangely moved. It reminded him of how lonely he was. And here was this innocent bunny sharing his captivity. Wow. If only he had the right teeth and shoulders, he might be Burt Lancaster in *The Birdman of Alcatraz.* He grinned widely and stretched his torso, and racked his memory for more examples of stuff about prisoners cheered up by a brush with wildlife; but beyond the little birdy in Byron's 'The Prisoner of Chillon', he couldn't think of much. He sighed and relaxed his face from the rather eerie Burt Lancaster impression. What about Job? he thought. Did not the God of the Hebrews send a bunny-rabbit to comfort Job, or was this yet another case of faulty recall? It was an interesting point to ponder. For example, if this rabbit were indeed engaged in work of a divine nature, would it really just sit there on the floor eating someone else's photo album? Osborne thought about this question for a bit, and decided he didn't have the proper theological qualifications for an educated answer.

'What have you got there?' he whispered instead. The rabbit took no notice and continued chewing. 'Let's see,' he said gently, and although he was a bit worried about what a rabbit might do to you if you interfered in the early stages of its main course, he tugged the album free and stood up to place it on a top shelf, noticing in passing that it said 'Our Weeding' in gold letters on the cover. Funny, thought Osborne fleetingly, as he popped it into the cupboard. He had met many gardening fanatics in his time, but none that kept a pictorial record of their anti-dandelion campaigns. Fancy that. 'Our Weeding'. He took it down and looked again. Oh yes, hang on, *'Wedding'*. Osborne laughed and shrugged. Well, 'Wedding' made a bit more sense, probably, but it was also somehow disappointing.

He opened it, just to be sure, and there it all was. Angela Farmer's summer wedding, in 1975, to Barney Jonathan, the comedian and TV producer. Cake-cutting, kissing, hand-holding, marquee, the works. Lots of famous supporting characters in the background, mostly London stage variety types with shiny noses, all in seventies period costume of big collars and flared trousers and platform boots (despite the heat). As Osborne flicked through the pages, Angela and Barney smiled inanely at each other; Barney opened countless champagne bottles; Barney lit a huge cigar, with a knowing wink. Osborne's trained eye picked out all the appearances of the shed, of course, even when it was not the main subject of the picture. He noticed it had been decked out in ribbons and used as a cold store for drinks. But the main thing that even Osborne could not ignore was the youthfulness of Angela – Angela looking fifteen years younger than she did today, and a lifetime more optimistic.

Osborne felt uncomfortable at the sight of Angela's bridegroom. Barney was possibly the only person Osborne had ever interviewed whose shed had subsequently received a scathing review in *Come Into the Garden*. In person, Barney had turned out to be precisely what you might expect from his roles on TV: good looking, well preserved, compulsively jokey, and a really mean bastard. It was at Barney Jonathan's house, actually, that the terrible business with the hyperactive child had taken place, when Osborne was locked in the shed for a laugh. If his resulting piece about Barney was one of his best observed and best written, there were two reasons for it: first, four hours gives you quite enough time to examine the contents of a shed; and second, Barney's character was so obnoxious that the writer needed to sew him up quite carefully, quoting him with deadly accuracy, so that he hanged himself with every word. Just mentioning his snide remarks about *Come Into the Garden*, for example, had been pretty useful for enlisting reader support against him; after all, you insult a magazine, you insult the person who's reading it.

Odd to think that Angela Farmer had married him. What an awful mistake. Turning the pages of the album, Osborne felt a tear roll down his face. He absent-mindedly stroked the rabbit, drew his legs up close, and for the next couple of hours studied the images, one after another, as the short November Tuesday lost its brightness and slowly began to wane.

Makepeace, by contrast, had not been idle. The sort of person who experiences an incandescent adrenalin rush not only from air disasters but from a harmless chat about the classics or a bit of mild criticism, this excitable dwarf had no difficulty summoning the gotta-get-outta-here energy that so noticeably eluded his chum. After an hour of frantic activity, therefore, in which his pony-tail wore loose and his sweaty hair hung down around his grim, determined face, he sat surrounded by a small armoury of improvised weapons (ingeniously utilizing paper-knives, shards of mirror, scissors, staples) and panted like a dog. He was not a pretty sight. Having inadvertently nicked his hands a few times in the course of handling broken glass, and then rubbed his face, he was now smeared with blood and dirt, which added not inconsiderably to the startling picture of miniature savagery he presented, reminiscent of something climactic from *Lord of the Flies*.

He decided to ransack the room. No point doing things by halves, after all. So he started knocking things over, sweeping documents off shelves, attempting to tear directories in half (abandoning this when it proved humiliating), and flinging Gordon's priceless work-in-progress computer disks around. It was only when he saw a set of files marked 'Digger' that he paused. Slavering slightly, he ripped open the first one, emptied the contents on the floor, and stirred the papers with his foot. Most of the documents seemed to be in computer code, all signed at the bottom by Gordon, but there was one that immediately caught his eye, because it was in the form of a letter. He knelt beside it to see.

> Dear Digger,
> You will find me in a country garden. I am an unknown quantity.
> My riddle is deep, and in the blue corner. Dig me up. I long for you.
> But remember the shirt of Nessus.

Makepeace couldn't help thinking, even in his excitement, that he was glad not to have Gordon for a pen-pal. To a devotee of *Digger*, of course, this letter made a sort of cryptic sense, and was merely a harmless stage in a game of clues. But to Makepeace it was further evidence that the boy was mad and dangerous. Gordon had lured Digger to a country garden ('Dig me up' was the rather ghastly invitation), but warned him about poisoned shirts that stick to your back and tear your flesh. Makepeace had to get out of here at once. Forget the heroics with the home-made machetes, perhaps he should just wriggle out of the window and climb down the drain-pipe. On the other hand, if he calmed down and thought about it, couldn't he see whether the key was still in the lock? Instead of fighting his way out, or crawling, there was just the faintest possibility he could unlock the door and walk out normally, down the stairs and out.

He peered through the lock and, sure enough, the key was there. Countless films had taught him what to do next. He slid a piece of paper under the door, poked the key with a paper-knife so that it fell on the paper, and then pulled it back under the door. Shame this didn't occur to me earlier, he thought, as he surveyed the devastation in the room and tried to staunch the bleeding of his hands with a wad of tissues. But on second thoughts, perhaps it was perfect this way. Those bastard perverts deserved it. Should he also scrawl 'PIGS' on the wall with his own blood, or would it be too sixties? He decided to have a go, but he ran out of free-flowing blood after 'PI'. Oh well, if this kid was such a mathematical brainbox perhaps he could distract himself by trying to understand PI, as so many had done before him. So, taking the 'Digger' letter with him, he left the room, locking it carefully and pocketing the key, and crept away downstairs.

In the shed, things were not harmonious.

'You've got nothing to go on,' barked Angela. 'That guy Osborne is a sweetheart. You nuts or something?' She paced up and down, smoking furiously, while Gordon and his dad exchanged glances.

'Tell her,' said Gordon's dad.

'You realize he could sue you for this?' she continued. 'Holding someone against his will is what is technically known as deep shit, you know that? Jesus, and he was so cute, too. We were really getting along.'

Gordon looked like he was going to burst into tears. Angela glared at him some more, and he felt wretched.

'So what you going to tell me? It better be good.'

Gordon pulled himself together. 'It's just that, well, you know that deal I did a couple of weeks ago? The one for the seaside postcards business? It included the magazine this Osborne chap works for, and I decided to close it down.'

'So? You feel guilty about a guy, you lock him up?'

'Well, and then he turns up here with his punchy sidekick, and they act very peculiar and shifty as though they're hiding something –'

'Big deal,' grouched Angela.

'And then the little one breaks into the B&B when we're out, and every time this Osborne sees me he leaps a foot in the air. Dad went back to check on the little one, but he's gone. And Dad had to break the door down to my office, and it's all mangled and covered with blood, and Dad's best hatchet has disappeared, and it's getting dark, and to be honest,' he gasped, 'I am really really scared.'

Angela huffed, but she also steadied herself against a wall. What the hell was all this blood and hatchet stuff?

'Where's the bunny?' she barked.

Gordon and his dad swapped dejected glances. 'We think, um ... ' they faltered, and cast grim looks towards the top of the house, where Osborne currently languished. They didn't need to finish.

'Oh no,' said Angela, 'oh swell.'

By the time Lillian arrived unnoticed on the scene at seven o'clock that evening, Angela and the Clarkes had made a decision. They would telephone Trent Carmichael, the celebrated crime writer, and ask him for some expert help. They would not contact the police. Through the locked door to Osborne's room, Angela had conducted a brief secret negotiation concerning the rabbit, with Osborne agreeing to let him out in return for some ham rolls, a few biscuits and a flask of tea. Osborne hastened to make it clear that he had not been holding the rabbit for purposes of ransom. The idea of taking a photo of the rabbit nervously holding a copy of today's newspaper would simply never have occurred to him.

'He seems like a nice rabbit,' he added lamely as he handed him over, catching Angela's eye and then looking away.

She felt terrible. 'I'm sorry about all this,' Angela said in an unusually meek voice.

Osborne, surprised, found himself reassuring her. 'Don't worry,' he said, 'I'm sorry too.'

She relocked the door and tiptoed away. Gordon and his dad would be furious to know she had talked with him. But then she tiptoed back again, and spoke very close to the door.

'Listen. Osborne. Whatever your name is. Can you hear me?'

'Yes.'

'Don't I know you from somewhere?'

'Somewhere, yes.'

'Aren't you going to tell me?'

'Well, the trouble is I can't remember.'

'Swell. You can't remember. That makes me feel much better.'

'I'm sorry.'

There was a pause, during which Osborne assumed she had gone away, so he started eating his tea. But she hadn't.

'Osborne, tell me, how about if I came along to see you later, and brought a bottle of wine or something? How would you feel about it? Would you think I was taking advantage?'

Osborne choked on a piece of ham roll.

'Forget it,' she said. 'Stupid, stupid.'

'No!' yelled Osborne, just catching her as she turned to go. 'That would be great. But, do you mean, just you and me?'

She looked hard at the closed door as if hoping to read its expression.

'Well, yes –'

'I mean, you wouldn't tell young Gordon?'

'Why, do you want Gordon along too?'

'No, no.'

'Thank goodness for that. But you shouldn't hate him, you know. He's a good kid. And he's really sorry about you losing your job. I think it's your little friend that worries him more than you. With good cause, by all accounts. Did you know he's on the loose with a hatchet, after ransacking Gordon's office and spraying the walls with blood?'

'What?' Osborne slumped to the floor. 'Oh God.'

'Osborne?'

Osborne made a small, high-pitched, inarticulate noise, something that sounded like '*Ing?*' but probably didn't signify anything other than despair.

Angela tapped on the door. 'You think he's dangerous, Osborne?'

'Oh God. *Ing?*'

'Speak to me.'

'I can't. *Ing?* Oh God. Sorry. *Ing?*'

'I'll come and see you later. I can bring some blankets and stuff. I know you're a nice man, Osborne. So tell me. All this locking you up is just a crazy misunderstanding, right?'

She waited, but no further words were forthcoming.

On the floor of the junk-room, Osborne lay in a curled position with a faraway look in his eyes, saying '*Ing?*' from time to time. He kept seeing this awful vision of Makepeace on the war-path, felling to the ground with a single blow from his hatchet all his natural foes – ranging from someone innocently pointing out that the lights on his bike weren't working, to a friendly pedant in a pub discussion mildly suggesting that his knowledge of North African nomadic ritual left a couple of smallish gaps.

Osborne felt he should open the window and warn the world that, in Honiton at the present moment, 'You're wrong there, you know' was the most dangerous expression a man could utter.

And now Lillian was here. She had booked herself a room in a pub, phoned a very confused Mister Bunny at home to tell him not to worry, and was now sitting in the dark in Angela Farmer's shed while deciding what to do next. She smoked and muttered compulsively. Much of her initial impetus, of course, had drained away in the course of the rather difficult train journey, but now that she had actually caught sight of Osborne at an upstairs window pacing about, she knew she had been right to come. Confronting Michelle must wait. If Lillian didn't get to the bottom of the G. Clarke stuff here and now, Osborne might suffer, and that would be terrible. Why was she there? Well, analysing her own motives required more effort than Lillian was prepared to give. However, it did occur to her that it was not just hatred of Michelle that had driven her to this peculiar behaviour. The cuteness of Osborne surely had something to do with it.

How Angela Farmer fitted into the scheme, she neither knew nor cared. Through the kitchen windows, she watched Ms Farmer in a family group with a big man and a red-haired youth, talking, making coffee, doing normal things (Lillian watched in agony; she would have killed for a cup-soup). These people seemed quite oblivious to the presence of an alien journalist two floors up. Lillian started to feel angry again. And where was Makepeace? There were quite a few things she wanted to say to him, when the time came.

She grimaced, took a final drag, stood up and chucked the cigarette into the back of the shed. Time to retrace her footsteps to the pub and consider a plan of action. Of course, she had no idea, in the dark, that Makepeace was lying in the shed behind her, asleep and unmoving, exhausted by a couple of hours' frenzied digging in Angela Farmer's garden. She did not know that he was sleeping the sleep of the vindicated, having located in the cold hard ground something that had been definitely hidden there – buried, as opposed to planted. And as she left the shed, and strode off into the night without a backward glance, she failed entirely to notice how the cigarette kindled into a small flame in the old, dry sheet music on which Makepeace slumbered, and then caught and burned and started to spread.

9

With the train service from Waterloo to Honiton scheduled to take a long and dreary three and a quarter hours, Michelle stared glumly out of the train window and contemplated how incredibly miserable the next portion of her life was going to be. The compartment smelled of ancient dust, the window was smeary as though painted with yellow glue, and moreover, with ten minutes till departure time, the worn and crusty seats were filling up with alarming speed. Michelle, unaccustomed to the brusqueness of Intercity etiquette, flinched and clenched her teeth as each new pinstriped bum wordlessly slapped down in a space she had fondly hoped would be empty. She was horrified. Who were all these men? Why were they so rude? And what possible reason could they have for catching a train to Honiton at half-past eight in the morning? When agreeing to make this journey, she had been comforted by a pleasant vision (admittedly founded on nothing more substantial than bluesy British Rail TV advertisements) that included an idea of relaxation and room to breathe. But the sad truth was that Michelle had worked in an office for too long. She did not know the first rule of British Rail travel: that if there is more than one cubic metre of space per passenger, something is deemed to be wrong and the service is cut.

The worst thing about the journey in prospect, however, was not the cattle-truck discomfort, nor the danger that someone would sit next to her eating an individual fruit pie without first inquiring whether she wanted some. It was that she and Tim now faced three and a quarter hours in which to bemoan their common predicament, which was simply this: they no longer had a magazine to sacrifice their lives to. 'No magazine' – what a strange combination of words. Perhaps that *was* glue on the windows, she thought – but her mind was wandering. She glanced around, pulled herself together, looked at her shoes, and faced facts. In the course of twenty-four hours *Come Into the Garden* had ceased to exist, and now she and Tim had been left, bewildered, sacrificing their lives to nothing.

It was a weird feeling. Each of them carried a business-like letter, received in the morning's post, informing them of Digger Enterprises' intention to cease publication of *Come Into the Garden* forthwith, *blah, blah,* sincere regret, *rhubarb* – but they still couldn't take it in. It seemed like nonsense. As she fought for breath, Michelle could not remember ever experiencing a shock of equal proportions. The day before, when the magazine's typesetters in Clerkenwell suddenly announced midway through the afternoon that they were laying down their tools, was a memory fresh as paint, and would remain so. When she thought of it, her mouth went all stiff, her shoulders came up around her ears, and she felt a terrible urge to hit someone.

Just like that, the typesetters had pulled the plug. The keyboard operatives stopped tapping; the compositors laid down their scalpels; and a few seconds' silence were respectfully (or was it ironically?) observed before attention turned routinely to the late news pages of *Pigswill Gazette* or *Marmalade Monthly*, or some such other grisly specialist publication. No matter that *Come Into the Garden* had run uninterrupted for fifty years. No matter that Michelle had given it the best years of her life. Later in the day, acting on his own initiative, a typesetter's clerical assistant with a nasty rash on his neck gathered up all the standing artwork from the *Come Into the Garden* pigeon-hole (the 'Me and My Shed' logo, the 'Dear Donald' in big loopy handwriting, the list of editorial staff that always appeared on page three underneath the Contents) and tipped them in a bin. Such is the passing of a little magazine.

Obviously, with typesetting a moribund trade, the managers of this little company were rightly dismayed to lose a nice regular job like *Come Into the Garden*. But on the other hand, the matter also had its compensations. The pleasure of finally telling Michelle over the phone precisely where she could stick her forebears and twinges and far-be-its and etceteras was so highly relished and coveted that, after a scuffle broke out at the coffee-machine between volunteers for the job, the men actually drew lots in the toilets. The lucky winner was a young paste-up artist called Jim – a relative newcomer, unfortunately, who had been allowed to take part in the draw only because the older blokes felt awkward about leaving him out. Fair and square he won it, but understandably the others were sore. By rights, the job should have gone to someone who had known Michelle much longer, who wanted it more badly; but such was fate. The hapless losers made the best of it by crowding around the office phone while youthful Jim made the historic call.

'We're not setting your stuff any more,' Jim told Michelle excitedly, in a rush, not savouring it at all. The other blokes shrugged; what a waste. Michelle, caught halfway through one of her arch how-I-hate-to-be-a-nuisance-pestering-you-for-co-operation complaints about the late arrival of proofs, paused for breath and considered what she had heard. 'Could I trouble you unforgivably and ask you to explain that last remark?' she asked. 'We're not setting it, you see,' said Jim, 'because you're going out of business.' Michelle gasped loudly and knocked over her bottles of nail varnish, so that her sub-editors looked up briefly from their work and bit their lips. 'But what am I going to do with all this copy?' she demanded crossly. At which she was surprised to hear the assembled typesetters, in the background, whoop with delight and crack up laughing. Ha ha, what could she do with that copy? Blimey, she walked right into that one.

Now she watched as Tim wiffled uncertainly down the platform to buy some coffees from the Waterloo concourse, and saw how thoroughly her life was tied up with *Come Into the Garden*. Just observing Tim's departing form, she realized she had never before encountered him outside the context of the office. Someone suggested having a drink after work once (at Christmas?), but Michelle had made an excuse and left; probably, Tim had done the same. At work, Tim looked different, somehow older; at work, they both knew what they were doing. She yearned to be back at her desk. A pile of features waited to be subbed, and she saw them in her mind's eye – all badly written, all straggly and formless, crying in the semantic wilderness for a decent sub to please, please show them the way (hoorah, a split infinitive) – and here she was, sitting on a train at the commencement of a fool's errand, thinking only of her own future. She felt guilty. Those features needed her. Her mission in life was to straighten them out.

Fifteen years working to a weekly production schedule would not be eradicated overnight. Wednesday morning, for Michelle, meant the arrival of next week's crossword (set since 1960 by an elderly cantankerous gaffer with dandruff, who signed himself 'Tradescant'); it meant final proofs of 'Ted's Tips'; the writing of the cover-lines by the editor (she rewrote them afterwards, he didn't seem to mind); and around lunchtime, it meant Osborne turning up in a flurry of string bags and oranges to write his terrible piece about celebrity sheds. Every week the same. The incontrovertible order of things. Whenever Michelle had taken holidays, it didn't matter where in the world she went, or how long she stayed away, she was aware hour by hour, almost minute by minute, of what ought to be happening at the office. Once, in a fabulous sea-front bar in Turkey, she had quite surprised her fellow Classical coach tour holiday makers by suddenly narrowing her eyes and snarling, 'That eleven-thirty messenger is early again, I just know it.'

So it was jolly hard to adjust to the idea that nothing whatever was happening in the office this morning, apart from a couple of volunteer subs answering the phones and dolefully dividing up the reference books to take home. Lillian had disappeared the previous afternoon, and Tim refused to tell her why. In fact he was particularly jumpy on the subject. But on hearing the terrible news from the typesetters – and then receiving his own ghastly letter of dismissal – he had been insistent that they travel immediately to meet with Digger Enterprises with a personal plea for time, or negotiated redundancy, or both; so here they were. Michelle was not optimistic that they could make any difference to the outcome, but agreed to go – partly, she realized on reflection, because she was too dazed to argue, and partly because, having never been to Honiton, she was curious to see it. Perhaps she would at last discover why 'Honiton, Devon' was always her first inspiration when writing spoof letters to either Osborne or the magazine.

She picked up the book she had brought for the journey (the new Trent Carmichael in hardback), but put it down quickly. By page forty-two she already had a fair idea that the gardener did it. She stared out of the window again and sighed. To think that only a week ago she had subbed Osborne's ropy Trent Carmichael piece so brilliantly. All those knowing references, all those clever puns; she had been born for this job, how could it possibly cease to exist? Morbid thoughts overwhelmed her. What would become of this highly specialized talent? Where could she take it? What was it worth? On the tube this morning she had come up with a superbly clever headline for a piece combining Orson Welles and patio furniture (should one ever crop up), yet all of a sudden there was no connection whatever between clever horticultural headlines and the price of sprouts. Her chin began to wobble. 'Nobody wants my *Sittings on Cane*' was possibly the saddest thought she had ever experienced.

'Not enjoying your book?'

She looked up in surprise to see a tanned, intense-looking man in a Barbour jacket and flat cap sitting opposite. Unlike everybody else on board, he must have sat down quietly, for he had completely escaped her notice. He looked familiar, but she couldn't think why. Outdoors-ish with his orangey-brown face and startling blue eyes, this man nevertheless had hands that were small, pink and soft; and his Barbour looked as if it had just come off the hanger in a Piccadilly outfitter's. No, she suppressed the idea as ridiculous; she didn't know him. After all, she reflected bitterly, unless he had worked for *Come Into the Garden* at some point in the past fifteen years, chances were obviously against it.

'So, not enjoying it, then?' he repeated, looking her challengingly in the eye and patting his corduroyed knees in a self-satisfied manner. He evidently thought this was funny. Some of the other passengers were pretending not to listen, and he seemed to be pleased by the attention, as though he deserved it.

'You ought to keep on with it, you know, the book. It might get better,' he said in quite a loud voice, and shot her a wink that said 'You know who I am, don't you?'

Michelle gave him a non-committal stare and noticed, with a certain revulsion, that his lips were a strange unnatural shade of salmon pink. Was this a chat-up line? Michelle sincerely hoped it wasn't. She peered exaggeratedly out of the window for Tim, but he was nowhere in sight.

'Oh look, my friend is just coming,' she said nevertheless, and – just for the sake of the fiction – waved pleasantly at a small bench in the middle distance.

Undeterred by her little ploy, however, the stranger reached forward and touched the book in her lap, the intimacy of the action sending a great shock-wave right through her body and out of her ears.

'That's mine actually,' he said, with a glamorous and rather insinuating smile. 'That's my book.'

Michelle pulled herself together, and stopped bothering to look for Tim – who was quite honestly going to miss the train if he didn't hurry.

'No, it isn't,' she said sharply. 'Look, I am on page forty-two.' She shuffled herself upright in her seat, and prepared for a fight.

'Oh no, I'm sorry, you misunderstand,' he said, still smiling. Looking at him, she couldn't decide whether he was handsome or vile. It was certainly a misfortune for a chap to have colouring so suggestive of cheap make-up from Woolworth's. 'What I meant was, well, *Murder, Shear Murder* was written by me. I take all the blame, ha ha. Guilty, your honour. I am the humble author.' He sat back and gave her a look that said 'Amazing, eh?' and waited for her reaction.

Michelle's eyes widened. Was this really Trent Carmichael? Author of *Dead for a Bucket*? What an extraordinary coincidence. She flipped the book over and looked at his picture, and then looked at him again. It was true. Of course, the man on the dustjacket was probably eight or ten years younger, and was pictured in black and white, and had evidently been told to assume a cold, murderous expression while resting on a shovel next to a freshly dug grave (it was rather a disturbing image, actually), but it was the same face, all right.

'Don't worry, I won't tell you how the story comes out,' he said teasingly (this sounded like a well-practised line). 'I won't disclose "who done it"!'

She laughed politely, wondering whether to mention she

had already formed a strong suspicion against the gardener. 'No, no,' she said, 'please don't tell. That wouldn't do at all.' Feeling awkward, however, she carried on. 'Actually I did guess the murderer in *S is for ... Secateurs!*' she said brightly, confused to find herself sounding gushing and inarticulate. 'Right at the very beginning, I thought that clever teenager, the girl, you know, the one who labels everybody, I guessed –' But she broke off, realizing rather late that crime writers aren't particularly interested to hear how easily you sussed their game.

She picked up the book and opened it again, but was confused about what to do next. Should she tell him she was a fan? That she had read every book? Should she mention the magazine article she had worked on? Or should she pretend to be so absorbed in *Murder, Shear Murder* that she couldn't stop for a chat, but must read on furiously, biting her nails? It was an unusual situation in which to find oneself. Her discomfort wasn't helped much, either, by Carmichael's rather eerie fixed smile. He seemed to be waiting for her to say something, something that was perhaps due to him as a famous person. But since she didn't know what it was, he was obliged to give her a hint.

'Would you like me to sign it for you?' He was leaning forward again, with that half-gruesome, half-engaging, proud-father smile. His body was so close she could smell his after-shave, which was earthy and rather strong.

'No, that's all right.'

'Really. It's no bother.' He had found a smart silver ballpoint pen in his inside pocket, and had popped it out, ready.

'No, really, I don't want you to.'

But he took the book and opened it at the title page. She noticed, with a flinch of annoyance, that he had carelessly lost her place. 'Now you're going to tell me your name.'

It wasn't a question. Michelle looked around for Tim again, but without much hope. He had evidently got caught up in a bullion robbery or something. At the back of the train, someone was blowing a whistle.

'Michelle,' she said at last, without much grace.

'That's a lovely name,' he said. 'Mmmmm. Michelle, Michelle, Michelle. Ma belle. Mmmmmm. Beautiful. Lovely.' He kept this up as he wrote in the book. When finished, he handed it back to her, and gave her a highly practised flash of famous-person charisma.

'Now, Michelle. Are you going to make it come true?' He pointed to the book, and she opened it at his inscription.

> To Michelle, whose delightful company and frankly unusual predilections have enriched my humble understanding of female desire. Our train journey was one I will never forget. Thanks so much for the memory.
>
> Your
> Trent Carmichael
> (CBE)

At which point, with Tim just hurrying through the ticket barrier balancing a couple of coffees and some slices of fruit cake on a wobbly paper tray, the train moved out of the station, leaving him behind.

Tim had not been caught up in a bullion robbery, he was merely phoning his ex-girlfriend Margaret for a bit of last-minute sympathy and support. However, compared with being tied up, blindfolded and bundled in the back of a hijacked Securicor van, the option of making voluntary contact with Margaret was probably only marginally less distressing. It was a stupid thing to do, of course, but he was desperate. Remembering that Margaret had a cousin and uncle in Honiton (Gordon something, an inventor, and his dad, an ex-fire-chief), Tim wildly decided that the journey in prospect was an adequate pretext to get in touch. How he thought he would obtain the yearned-for sympathy and support is less easily explained, since he ought surely to have recollected that Margaret possessed talent and inclination for neither. But he phoned her, the poor sap, he did. He even missed his train in this forlorn hope of a few kind words.

Margaret's readings in psychology were extremely handy for a person disinclined to mollycoddle, which is perhaps why she took up the subject in the first place. It was rather neat: for Margaret, psychology meant never having to say you're sorry; you could hurt people and then, with a single bound, get away with accusing them of textbook insecurity. Objective reality is an illusion, she reckoned; fulfilled and unfulfilled desires account for everything. Thus, if someone were to phone her up at half-past eight in the morning (say) and tell her he was jolly upset about his magazine closing, she could argue that secretly he must have wanted it to happen. Tim unfortunately had forgotten about all this when he made his last-ditch call from the end of Platform 12. He had forgotten, in particular, that Margaret would reiterate her usual theory that his feelings were all connected with his mother, with 'pain of separation' and something anal to which she sometimes referred darkly but never satisfactorily explained. Amazing that he could have forgotten. Less amazing, perhaps, how it all came flooding back.

'Listen,' he protested after a couple of minutes, almost in tears at her refusal to accept the straightforward case of the matter. 'I've lost my job. It's real. It's happened. My job!' He was obliged to shout, so that he could hear his own voice above the ambient station noises.

'"Job",' repeated Margaret playfully. She was enjoying this. Just out of the shower, she was towelling her hair while keeping an eye on the weather forecast on Breakfast TV. 'That's a very telling choice of word, Tim. It makes me wonder whether you mean your big job or your little job.'

Tim felt wretched. Was there really something psychologically revealing about using the word 'job'? Was it this anal thing again?

'All right, then, my *position*.'

Margaret laughed. 'Position' was clearly no improvement. Tim looked at his watch and started worrying whether he really had time for all this.

'How about *post*?'

'Ha!'

Tim gave up. It suddenly struck him that she might be writing this down.

'Still keeping Post-it notes in business?' asked Margaret. Now that she had started, she seemed to be relishing the chat.

'I don't know what you mean.'

'I thought of you last week when the *Independent* went up by five pence,' she said. 'God, how I remember the trauma from last time. I told everybody on the course about it, and they couldn't believe it, they thought I was making it up. We had a really good laugh. So what did you decide?'

'I decided not to let it worry me,' he said, lying.

'Gosh, well done.'

If this was a stupid conversation to miss a train for, it was also a stupid one to get upset about, yet quite out of nowhere Tim suddenly realized he was crying. Two huge tears welled up behind his specs, and involuntarily he felt all the muscles in his face dissolve.

'Do you ever miss me?' he asked.

'Of course.' Margaret was now brushing her long dark hair, deliberately creating static electricity in it, so that she could hold the brush to one side and observe the way the hair lifted up, defying gravity, reaching out feebly for support. She put the brush down, and the hair collapsed.

'I miss you,' said Tim.

'Of course you do.'

'I mean it, I really miss you.'

'And I mean it, too. *Of course you do.*'

'I can't live without you.'

'That's nonsense.'

Tim choked on a sob, and noticed that his money was running out.

'Better go,' he said, 'I'm worried about missing my train.'

'That's typical of you, Tim,' said Margaret, to the sound of a disconnected line. 'That's absolutely textbook.'

As soon as she put down the phone, she grabbed for a large box on a shelf marked 'TIM' and hauled it down. Efficiently she made a few notes on a scrap of paper, circling the words 'job', 'position' and 'post' in green pen, and carefully noting the time and date at the top in blue. She was getting good at this, she reflected; the 'TIM' box was almost full. It would soon be time to convert all the research into a ground-breaking casebook study and unleash her ex-boyfriend's obsessive-compulsive disorder on the waiting public. She could see it now, the scene in the bookshop, with her signing copies of *Tim: How I Lived with a Loony*, just like her old buddy Trent Carmichael sometimes did. Margaret's mum once mentioned, tentatively, that perhaps Tim's identity ought to be disguised when the book was written, but Margaret had set her straight about this, impressing on her the demands of proper scientific practice. 'It's got to be authentic!' she declared, her eyes passionate. 'Don't forget I only lived with Tim in the first place because he promised to provide such fantastic material. Do you think I would compromise my own academic integrity by telling anything less than the exact truth?' Hearing the case put like that, Margaret's mum – who had been told about her own inadequacies enough times to know when she was out of her depth – decided to rest her case. As Margaret had so rightly pointed out on numerous occasions, she should just count herself lucky that no companion volume called *Mum: Every Detail of What's Wrong with the Stupid Old Bat* had, as yet, got past the planning stage.

Margaret phoned up British Rail and asked for the train times to Honiton. This was just what the book needed, Tim driven to misery and madness by the loss of all his routines at a single blow. She couldn't afford to miss it, even though the place made her slightly uncomfortable. Gordon and his dad were pussy-cats, it wasn't them she was worried about. It was whatsername, Barney's ex-wife, up the road. Ten years ago, when Margaret was fourteen, there had been a bit of an incident in Barney's garden – ever since when that creepy Trent Carmichael had referred to her as his 'partner in crime'. But it was all a long time ago – just before Gordon and his dad moved to Dunquenchin, and just before Carmichael wrote his breakthrough bestseller *S is for ... Secateurs!* Cleverly, Trent had persuaded Barney's wife to star in the TV version, just for his own (and Margaret's) private amusement. One day she planned to write a book entitled *Trent: Psychopaths Do It but They Don't Get Involved*, but obviously not just yet.

10

On Wednesday morning, the *shedus mirabilis* lay in ruins.

'Oh my good giddy bugger uncle,' said Osborne in alarm, as he drew the thick heavy curtains to Angela's bedroom at eight o'clock, and saw the devastation. Outside, the day was lovely – bright winter sunshine, Cambridge-blue sky, leafless oaks rocking gently in the breeze. But what really caught one's attention from the vantage-point of the first-floor master bedroom, what really socked you in the mincies (as it were), was this smouldering half-collapsed wooden structure from which white smoke and twirling ash were belching, rather as though it had just exploded.

Osborne turned to look at Angela, still comatose, and wondered how he should break the news. Charred and tattered fragments of her favourite old sheet music were taking impulsive little sideways runs across the garden, settling briefly, and then somersaulting and darting off to impale themselves on rose bushes.

The double-glazed bedroom window foiling Osborne's powerful impulse to open it, he just clawed feebly at the glass like a trapped kitten. He didn't understand: how could this conflagration have gone unnoticed from indoors? True, as he looked back at Angela, her bedside table strewn with empty champagne bottles, knocked-over glasses, and ravaged packets of prophylactics, perhaps it wasn't quite such a mystery. In fact, now he came to scratch his addled bonce and give it some sensible thought, he did remember the red light flickering in the night, because, yes, he had drawn attention to it at a key moment. Angela had been sitting astride him at the time (doing an expert high-bouncing impression – quite belying her years, actually – of an oscillating suction pump), and he remembered how, in all the mounting tremendous smelly wump-wump shrieking willy-frenzy, he had gazed in transcendent wonder at a thin sliver of beautiful red-and-yellow light patterns dancing on the ceiling in the dark.

'Is that the Northern Lights?' he had shouted deliriously, pointing upwards. 'Or is it me?'

Angela, concentrating rather hard on something else at this juncture, didn't answer. Instead, she pushed her hands harder against his chest, dug in her nails, arched her back, squeezed a secret muscle, and stepped up the tempo.

'Anje-ler,' he had gasped, 'is it – me? – Or is it – Oh God – Northern – Aagh – Northern –?'

'That's not the Northern Lights!' she yelled, as suddenly her whole body whiplashed and convulsed in a huge, melting, electrifying spasm. 'That's – Oh *God!* – that's *Manderley!*'

There had been several other climaxes, but the Daphne du Maurier was honestly the hottest and the best. If Osborne was a bit hazy about the exact order of events before and after this, however, it was not surprising, given the amount of alcohol they had jointly consumed. Angela had unlocked his door at 8 p.m., just after insisting that Gordon and his dad return to Dunquenchin ('Go home, I'll be fine, I've got – er, lots of catching up to do,' she said, choosing her words carefully). Having taken Osborne straight to her room, she immediately opened the champagne, knocked some half-chewed scripts off the quilt, talked eagerly with him about sheds and deadlines and house-sitting for half an hour as though honestly she had no idea what was going to happen next, and then suddenly she was undressing him and they were doing wild, intense, all-night impressions of suction pumps, piston engines, and Old Faithful in the Yellowstone National Park. Osborne still couldn't recall where he had met her before, but it was ceasing to matter. She was wonderful. And the quite amazing thing was, she seemed to like him, too.

'Hey, did we do that?'

She had appeared beside him in a large T-shirt printed with 'BEHIND EVERY SUCCESSFUL WOMAN THERE IS A RATHER TACKY DIVORCE', and was staring at the shed.

'I guess we did,' she shrugged, and kissed him on the neck.

A great advantage of their happy deluge of bodily fluids was that, paradoxically, it had given them the opportunity to clear a few things up. In between taking fortifying slugs of Moët et Chandon and tracing affectionate patterns in spilled fizz on one another's unfamiliar skin, they had talked, naturally enough, about how Osborne had so far veered from the road most travelled that he had wound up locked in a sitcom star's upstairs cupboard with a voracious rabbit, in mortal fear of a teenage psychotic computer prodigy dressed in a see-through frock. Put like that, it took a bit of working out. But Osborne explained about the letters, and Makepeace's suspicions of Gordon (it all sounded rather pathetic, now); meanwhile, Angela reassured him that Gordon was shifty only because he felt guilty about the closing of the magazine, and because he had temporarily made the natural mistake of thinking Osborne and Makepeace were hit-men.

'What's this book like?' Osborne asked now, picking up *Murder, Shear Murder* from the floor.

'Oh, the usual thing. Inspector Greenfinger investigates: "I expect you're all wondering why I called you together in this potting shed with a strimmer, a Geoff Hamilton video and a stopwatch." I was in one of his things on TV once – I was the brave, red-herring, alcoholic wife whose husband was bonking a Lolita in the greenhouse. I wasn't saddled with a tulip in those days, or God knows what that crazy guy would have made of it. Trent was real impressed with the piece you wrote, incidentally – but no, I told you that already.'

'I don't usually read detective novels,' said Osborne.

'You don't?' Angela looked a bit surprised. 'Listen, why don't you read the first few pages of this one while I go to the bathroom, and tell me who you think did it. Five minutes should give you ample time. And then we'll have an enormous breakfast and phone the Clarkes and tell them there's nothing –' She stopped abruptly.

Osborne looked up confused from his perusal of the first paragraph. 'Well, it's a wild guess at this stage,' he said, 'but what about the gardener?'

Angela punched herself rather hard in the abdomen and let out a groan. 'Oh for heaven's sake, I just remembered. We called Trent last night. He's *coming*.'

'What? To tell you who did it? Couldn't you just read to the end?'

'No, he's coming to investigate you. Well, you and the other guy. What the hell am I going to tell him? And what the hell am I going to tell him about the goddam shed?'

Gordon had not slept much. The idea of Makepeace on the loose and Osborne forcibly holed up with the rabbit was not the thing to aid carefree slumbers; meanwhile, he knew that today's closure of *Come Into the Garden* would make him deeply unpopular with a further group of people, whose identities he didn't even know. In the night he sighed a lot, tossed and turned, punched his pillow into different shapes, noticed a warm glow in the dark morning sky (but thought nothing of it), and finally climbed the stairs to his office, cleared a space in the chaos, and – for the first time in two years – took refuge in *Digger*, immersing himself in virtual reality from about five o'clock in the morning until he could speak to his dad at eight. By normal *Digger* standards, three hours was a short session, but it was highly distracting, as it was intended to be. Mentally, Gordon dug and laboured and dug again, and tried to piece together the bits that came up. If there was nothing in the real world Gordon wished to think about at present, least of all did he wish to contemplate the imminent arrival of the legendary Trent Carmichael, whom he considered an absolute gasbag. To him, the idea of inviting that charlatan down from London as if he were Sherlock Holmes was so absurd he wanted to scream. But alas, he had been outvoted. Both Dad and Angela evidently thought highly of Carmichael's piddling, minuscule abilities; not only were they somehow impervious to his creepy, patronizing tone, but Angela seemed almost to *like* it. Considering that she could normally spot a phoney at twenty paces, this was completely inexplicable.

That Carmichael was a creep, a phoney and all the rest, Gordon had no doubt. Years ago, when the Clarkes had first moved to Dunquenchin, Gordon overheard him whispering to cousin Margaret in the dining-room, and was terribly shocked. First, he disliked the intensely familiar tone (Margaret would have been only fifteen at the time); but more importantly, he hated the way they laughed at Angela behind her back. Angela's marriage had just broken up; it was awful that they should joke about it. Ever since, the very mention of Carmichael made Gordon alternately bristle and sulk. So when Angela had yesterday described the plot of *Murder, Shear Murder*, with its ginger-haired young victim, it was not surprising he took it so personally. Carmichael, for all his magisterial tone, was at heart a touchy blighter, who knew perfectly well that Gordon distrusted him. It would give him nothing but pleasure to stick his young rival in a crime novel as an early casualty, skewered to the deck with a wooden-handled Spear & Jackson's.

Gordon shuddered, turned off his computer and glanced out of the window. It was light now. With the help of *Digger*, he had made it through the dawn. As usually happened when he unlocked himself from virtual reality, he saw the everyday world as strange, flat, weirdly coloured and slightly sinister. Which was why, when he first noticed the strange tall woman in a shocking-pink coat staring up at the house, smoking a cigarette and muttering to herself, he wasn't convinced she was real. She was holding a large file of papers under her armpit. 'Oi!' said Gordon, opening the window, 'what do you want?' But by the time he looked down again the shocking-pink lady had gone.

'So then I wrote *S is for ... Secateurs!*,' chuckled the humble author, shouting to be heard above a set of points, 'and after that I never looked back!'

Michelle, pointedly consulting her watch as the Carmichael monologue clocked up its fifty-fifth minute, smiled faintly and gave up trying to get a word in. She could certainly appreciate that Trent Carmichael was a never-look-back sort of person. The trouble, unfortunately, was that he was evidently a never-glance-sideways person, too, with possibly the worst case of tunnel vision she had ever in her life encountered. This absence of peripheral eyesight was literal – in that he didn't seem to notice anything not directly in front of him (the ticket collector was obliged to bend down and speak straight into his face) – but it was also metaphorical. Trent Carmichael ploughed a very straight furrow, narrative-wise, and refused to be distracted by any question a polite interlocutor might pose. 'So when was this?' Michelle might ask; or 'So why are you on this train?' But Carmichael told his story in strict chronology, and without deviation from a fixed agenda. Thank God we have at last reached the mega-success of *S is for … Secateurs!*, thought Michelle. The rest is surely history.

'But that's enough about me,' he said, with a visible effort. 'Tell me about yourself. Tell me what *you* think about me!'

Michelle was so surprised, she just shook her head.

'Don't you want to tell me all about yourself? I am disappointed, Michelle. In fact, I am hurt. People generally do, you see. Because I'm an author, and they want me to immortalize them in prose.'

'Well, if you're an author, why don't you just make me up?' said Michelle heatedly. 'Why do you need me to tell you anything? Besides, how could you know enough about me from a chat on a train to put me in a novel?'

'Ah, but you don't understand. The Michelle I will write about is not the person whose life you would describe. When I put you in a novel, I have the power to take liberties with you. I can peel back your layers, rip you open like a fig; do you understand? And you will surrender, joyfully. What shall I make of you, Michelle? I think I shall make you a flirtatious, gardening sex-kitten in thick gloves who – oh, what shall I say? – who likes to tie men's arms with garden twine and stroke their nipples with a pitchfork.'

'What?' Michelle almost screamed. How on earth did he know about the pitchfork? Or Osborne's nipples? Was this man a mind-reader, a blackmailer, what?

Carmichael raised an eyebrow and pretended not to notice the strength of her reaction. This was always his favourite bit, when he met new women, teasing them with kinky scenarios and gauging the reaction, while also trying out new plot ideas. Being a naturally parsimonious person, he liked the idea of killing two birds with one stone; the economy of effort gave him pleasure. Plus his success rate was uncanny, since sometimes (as with Michelle, apparently) he could hit home at once with dead-eye accuracy.

'Or I could make you the victim, if you prefer,' he continued, giving her time to collect herself. 'I don't know, buried alive, perhaps? Or covered with beer and slobbered to death by marauding snails? People often ask me, you know, why I choose the garden as my homicide arena, they think it might be restricting. But gardens are dangerous. They are also filled with the violent struggle of life, as flowers are forced to bloom wide and shriek with colour in their last gasp. And besides, as I always say to interviewers, it's just *right* to die in a garden. You know the old rhyme, I suppose:

'The kiss of the sun for pardon,
The song of the bird for mirth,'

– here he paused for the full sinister effect of his italics –

'*One is nearer to God in a garden*
Than any place else on earth.'

Michelle did indeed know the old rhyme, but found it hard to associate the kiss of the sun and the song of the bird with Carmichael's relentless fixation with sticking Wilkinson Sword gardening tools into people's necks. However, since the erotic mental picture of Osborne's little pink nipples standing out on a milk-white, goose-fleshy, hairless chest was now making her feel a bit sticky, she was probably not in a position to criticize.

'I expect you are wondering why I called you all together, I mean, sorry, whoops, why I am on this train,' Carmichael smirked, pleased with his own joke. 'I am bound for Honiton, in the county of Devonshire, my dear, just as you are (I stole a look at your ticket), because my deductive talents have been summoned by a Miss Angela Farmer. She has a little mystery that requires a solution.'

At the name Angela Farmer, Michelle frowned a little, but he didn't notice.

'Nothing murderous, so far as I understand, so please don't alarm yourself on my account. I'm sure I shall be perfectly safe. No, the lady is acquainted with my fine sleuthing instincts, so naturally, having a little problem with a, let's see –' here he opened a small leather-bound notebook and peered at some notes, '– oh yes, a crazed journalist with a hatchet, she thought I might investigate.'

Michelle gulped. Could he mean Osborne? After all, Osborne had visited Angela Farmer this week. But what was this stuff about a hatchet?

'You wouldn't know the publication *Come Into the Garden*, I suppose?' he said.

'No,' she said, her face glowing hot, 'I mean, oh no. I don't think so. What is it?'

'It's a rather ghastly little magazine, quite frankly, with a tiny circulation, the sort of thing one's mother used to read, if you know what I mean. Full of old-fashioned tips that the average gardener knows already, completely behind the times. You sometimes get a free packet of seeds. But they have a regular item about celebrity sheds which isn't too bad – I know, I know, *sheds!* – but luckily they do manage to attract some stunning high-class names sometimes, some *really* top people, if you know what I mean. For example, they asked *me* –'

'I see. And now Angela Farmer –?'

'Yes, now Angela Farmer.'

'I think I understand,' said Michelle, rather glad now that Carmichael had so utterly dominated the conversation. As far as he was concerned, she could be anyone; he knew nothing about her. 'So when they ask you about your shed,' she asked innocently, 'does it have to be particularly interesting? Or must you just fabricate stories about the cat being locked in it?'

Carmichael regarded Michelle solemnly, and then reached over and grabbed her hand. He spanked it lightly, and when she drew a sharp breath to complain, he put his fingers on her mouth. They smelled, but she didn't react. She just tensed up as he whispered to her.

'You are a remarkable woman. Michelle, and I am sure you remember what I wrote in your book. So perhaps now you would care to accompany me to the buffet car, or possibly the guard's van, and we'll find out what you *really* like?'

Lillian was on the phone to Mister Bunny. She didn't have an idea in her head to tell him, so worked round the problem with her usual panache.

'Oh, oh, bunny ever so sorry,' she said, with a big childish shrug which really helped the performance, even over the phone. 'Bunny just *can't* come home to Bunnyland right now. Just *can't*, bunny. Not poss. Poor bunny. Shame, shame, shame.'

Then she listened for a bit, while he gently asked the important questions – 'Where are you?' and 'What on earth are you up to?' and 'Where do we keep the bin-liners?' – at the end of which she took the conversation straight back to Bunnyville.

'Miss you, bunnykins, miss you like ever so. I had a rotten night-night, you know, without the ted-babies and the wombats.'

This was clever, since Lillian knew the mere mention of lonely wombats would be more than Mister Bunny could bear. She was right. Before he knew it, he was saying that the poor little ted-babies and wombats had missed her, too; and that ted-baby Dexter needed wrapping up against the cold again, despite being a white bear presumably acclimatized to polar regions. Lillian suggested a red knitted scarf, and together they discussed its merits. And before long, Lillian's money ran out, which was a kind of blessing, whichever way you look at it.

Thus beguiled (as always) by the charms of Bunnyland, Mister Bunny hung up before realizing he still didn't know where his wife was, or what she was doing, or who she was with. Furthermore, if he wanted a bin-liner, he was buggered.

For her own part, much as she loved Mister Bunny, Lillian was glad the conversation was over. Admittedly Mister Bunny was a real good hubby, and their home was full of furry love and squirrel cuddles, and ted-babies snuggled in special knitted scarves; but on the other hand, sometimes in a secret part of herself, Lillian thought the hell with this, I'm forty-two. It never occurred to her that Mister Bunny (or whatever his real name was, she'd temporarily forgotten) might secretly think the same, and that perhaps a teddy amnesty followed by a big teddy bonfire might work wonders for the marriage. Alas, just as it is possible to stand so close to a wood that you can only see trees, so it is possible to be so densely involved in the dark depths of the marital bunny-wunnies that you just worry that Dexter the white bear is feeling the cold on wintry nights, or that he gets depressed during *Panorama*.

Better call the office, she thought, and make up some excuse. As she punched the number (she was using the pay-phone at Honiton station) she had this horrible presentiment that Michelle would answer and make things awkward. But instead of the snappy Michelle, a very quiet and unfamiliar voice answered, claiming to be somebody called Clement. Well, naturally Lillian denied all knowledge of anybody called Clement, and things turned a bit nasty until it was finally established to her satisfaction that Clement was in fact a sub who had been working at *Come Into the Garden* for two or three years, and that she ought to remember him because he once obligingly polished her post-sorting tongs when they lost their sparkle. At which point she decided to be gracious about it.

'Look,' she started to say, 'whoever you are, and you shouldn't be so bloody nondescript in my opinion, if you want people to take any notice, just tell Tim that I shan't be in today but I expect to be back by Friday –'

But he interrupted her. Didn't she get her letter this morning? At home? Telling her the magazine was closing? That *Come Into the Garden* was no more? 'We found out yesterday,' he said, 'after you'd – er, what was it, gone out or something – and then today we all got letters from Digger Enterprises in Honiton. They've decided to close us down.'

Lillian staggered.

'Michelle and Tim have gone by train to Honiton this morning to see if they can talk Mr Clarke out of it, beg for time, you know. But in the meantime, Ferdie and I thought we'd start sharing things out in the office, and actually it's good you called because Ferdie wanted to know whether that standard lamp was going begging, or whether it was yours.'

'It's mine,' she snapped. 'You leave that standard lamp alone.'

'We didn't think we wanted to take anything, but it's funny, once you start thinking about it, and looking around, you want to take home all the chairs and standard lamps and – sorry, I'm running on, and you're not well, this is terrible. Are you all right, Lillian? Honestly, we won't touch any of your stuff until, um, at least tomorrow. Anyway, we'll be here if you need us, although obviously we'll go quite early this afternoon because there's no work to do, it's really odd, especially without Michelle ...'

And so he went on. Lillian didn't know what surprised her most, this appalling news about the magazine, or the fact that a sub called Clement (for heaven's sake) could get words out in such quantities. But it was all, all of it, very hard to absorb. The fax she had received at the office was no hoax, then. This G. Clarke really existed. He was not just Michelle's dangerous *alter ego* who had wicked designs on Osborne; he had bought *Come Into the Garden* and closed it down.

Suddenly the full force of it hit her, and she felt her face burn with indignation. Fifteen years! After all she'd done! A decade and a half of back-breaking toil had just been tossed aside, flung in her face, taken for the high jump, or another more exact metaphor that would possibly strike her later. Fifteen child-bearing years of thanklessly answering that phone, sorting post, nodding at people with stupid names like Clement, trying to keep their spirits up with friendly chat. All down the Swanee, out the window, down the toilet.

She had done *everything* for that magazine. And here was her future. On the bonfire with the rest of the flop-eared bunnies. Bitterly she remembered how she had once put a note on the stationery cupboard saying, 'Tell me when you remove things from this stationery cupboard, I am not psychic you know', and had a row with Michelle about it. The things she had put up with from Michelle! Just in the cause of keeping the office running smoothly. To think she had given herself so entirely to an enterprise only to be chucked in the bin, let out with the bathwater, thrown to the wolves, cut loose from the dock. It was no good, the phrase wasn't coming. It probably required a calmer state of mind.

Should she call up Mister Bunny again, and tell him what was going on? No, better not. He had Dexter's chill to worry about. But if she were going to stay in Honiton and get Osborne released from his upstairs prison (the Michelle and Tim mission to G. Clarke could wait till later, and Honiton was a big place), it was obviously imperative that she make a friend on the inside, and she rather thought the young lad with the ginger hair was the ideal fellow. He had an honest face, he appeared to be a confidant at Angela Farmer's house and, best of all, he seemed to live at a B & B, so she could move in without it looking suspicious. (Usually it does look suspicious if you move into someone's house and make friends with them afterwards.)

Lillian felt her resolution grow to bursting-point within her. These bastards wouldn't grind her down. She could go undercover, calling herself – um, Miss Dexter, yes; Miss Dexter from the teddy business. Which had the obvious virtue of being easy to remember.

As she made her way to Dunquenchin, grimly she lit a cigarette and thought how hard it was for a woman in her position, with such a fantastic level of commitment, to be jettisoned, ditched, dislodged, discarded, put out with the cat, stubbed out like a fag-end. It was curious, this; but for the first time in her entire life, Lillian felt the lack of a thesaurus.

11

Late that night at Dunquenchin, all was silent save for the muffled keyboard thumpings of Margaret's lap-top word processor as she sat up in bed with her specs on, an old blue cardigan pulled around her shoulders, and worked with fanatical concentration on the day's events. Pigs in muck don't usually make notes about the experience, but in most other respects – especially the snorting with pleasure – the resemblance between Margaret at Dunquenchin and a pig in muck was actually quite striking. So much to write, she thought, as her nimble fingers danced and flew over the flat grey keys at midnight; so much to write, tra-la, tra-la, diddle-dee; so little alternative to damned hard work in this relentless pursuit of excellence. She frowned and licked her lips and, with a huge effort at selflessness, pitied all the poor little people in the world of psychological research who suffered the current misfortune not to be her.

Such a burden. Not for the first time, she pondered the enormous responsibility she owed to her talent. How could any single person, even a noted brainbox such as herself, hope to assimilate and organize all the extraordinary tell-tale psycho hang-ups she had witnessed today? Sometimes she wished she could subdivide herself, in the manner of an amoeba, to form two identical Margarets, or four, or sixteen, or 256, all tapping away at their lap-tops in Busby Berkeley formation, all equally dedicated to blasting their insights into the waiting world. Ah, the truth was clear to see: in common with the poet Keats (but with arguably less cause for regret), Margaret had fears that she might cease to be before her pen had glean'd her teeming brain.

Fortunately, however, the other 255 lap-top-thumping Margarets were as yet babes unborn; and uniqueness was still one of the nicest attributes you could ascribe to her. 'There's only one Margaret Sexton, and I'd know her anywhere,' Trent Carmichael had commented aloud, with an interestingly ambivalent choice of greeting, when he recognized her voice from the dining-room of Dunquenchin that afternoon. She and Tim had travelled on the same train, not knowing it; but immediately on arrival in Honiton she persuaded him to join her at her uncle's, so here they were: Margaret springing forward to be greeted by a tanned, handsome Silver Dagger Award winner with big white teeth; Tim hanging back in the hall, looking thin, pale, bothered and demoralized. He had never noticed it before, but suddenly the sleeves and armholes of his jumper were so tight he could hardly breathe. It hadn't helped his spirits much, either, that Margaret introduced him to her nice cousin Gordon by reminding everybody of that oft-related, character-pigeonholing incident from his childhood when he dug up those bloody bulbs.

Tim had good reason for his mood of despair on arrival at Dunquenchin. Not only was he out of a job, uncertain as to the whereabouts of his chief sub and secretly worried almost to distraction about whether he had locked his front door properly, but on the way from the station he had volunteered to carry Margaret's dead-weight briefcase, and the effort had nearly killed him. Unknown to him, alas, this bag contained Margaret's entire TIM file, complete with diagrams, photos, computer print-out and even some specimens of his famous Post-it notes. This explained why Margaret, watching him wrestle innocently and pink-faced with the bag, considered the whole thing absolutely hilarious. Oh dear, she thought later in bed (removing her specs briefly to wipe her watering eyes), she was going to miss studying Tim.

> Tim's behaviour shows all the classic signs of deterioration [she wrote with lightning speed] – the anal retentive obsessive–compulsive control freak loses his routines at a single blow, and his personality implodes. It is happening already, and it is fascinating. What worries me is whether my own presence on the scene – as his 'ex-girlfriend' – will in any way interfere with the natural course of his inevitable breakdown; after all, science would not thank me for supplying the cause of his bearing up and surviving! However, I noticed that he burst into tears when we came upstairs to our separate rooms at bedtime, so perhaps I am worrying about nothing. I do hope I am not becoming neurotic! To be fair to myself, I may in fact be helping to nudge him off into the abyss, which is reassuring. I don't believe in rigging experiments, but there is surely nothing unethical in helping him along his destined path.

Margaret took a sip of cold Oxo from a brown mug, nibbled a piece of cheese and stared briefly at the wall before continuing.

> It was a surprise to see Trent here, especially with the peculiar new girlfriend. A bit old for him, though, or so I would have thought, from my own experience. Talking of which, I notice he is still using that picture I took of him, the one of the burials in Angela Farmer's garden, on the dustjacket of his books, so he hasn't forgotten our little pact. He pretended to be pleased to see me, but he knows I could ruin him tomorrow if I wanted to! Tee hee.

On the other hand, since I did unintentionally provide him with his first and best plot – has he ever done anything better, or more creepy, than S *is for ... Secateurs!?* – he ought to be jolly grateful. The new book isn't so good by a long chalk, except that, to be fair, when you get to the end, and find out that the gardener did it (the gardener!), it comes as a complete surprise.

But the main thing is Tim's reaction. There we are, middle of the afternoon, and here's Carmichael in the dining-room snogging this unknown woman over a batch of scones, and Tim just stands there gaping. I say something like, 'This is my old friend Trent Carmichael,' but Tim says nothing, he points at the woman – who's somehow got clotted cream on her neck, and lipstick all over the place, and buttons half undone – and he makes stifled baby-like 'Mm ... Mmm ... ' noises. The others don't know what to make of this, but I do. He is obviously traumatized by displays of sexuality! Compounded with this he also hates the sight of cream (mother's milk! mother is a cow?!); or JAM (good grief! red stuff! menstrual blood! oozing thickly!). Either way, he cried for his mummy ('Mm ... Mmm ... !') in a very gratifying way.

'This is Michelle,' says Trent. The woman glances at Tim, and is so struck by the incredulous look he gives her that she actually runs out of the room. 'I work with that woman,' Tim confides to me, in a whisper, as we make our way upstairs. 'Of course you do,' I say in my best bedside manner, thinking *He must relate the event to himself*! 'But on the other hand, Tim,' I said calmly, 'you are probably having just a teeny bit of a breakdown, because of getting the sack. And as for that, well, let's remember that you don't actually work with *anyone* any more!' It was a kindness to mention it.

I do believe I am uncovering a completely new syndrome. I could call it post-traumatic redundancy syndrome, and it could form the whole second half of the book. Later in the afternoon, when we went out to buy a toothbrush for Tim (he worries about his TEETH!), we passed a woman on the street, she was wearing a pink coat and carrying a big white toy bunny-rabbit in broad daylight. I pointed her out myself, just for the sake of a laugh. But 'Good heavens,' said Tim, clutching the wall of the bank. 'I *work with that woman.*' 'No you don't,' I said, 'you ought to get a grip.' 'I do,' he insisted. 'If you want, I'll ask her,' I offered, but the woman took one look at Tim and disappeared. He is scaring people, terrorizing complete strangers. *It is possible he will have to be hospitalized.* Anyway, she dropped the rabbit and Tim picked it up – which is terrific stuff for the case-study, as I hardly need mention. In the spirit of scientific discovery, I took a photo.

For the rest of the afternoon, I pointed out more people that Tim might claim to have worked with (a couple of dogs and cats, too, just in case), but the delusion seemed to have passed. However, just before bedtime I heard him shout something that sounded like 'Make peace!' from his room, and of course I ran in, because if he was starting to yell stuff, I didn't want to miss it. 'You want to make peace?' I said, hardly able to contain my excitement. 'That's terribly interesting, you know, Tim.' 'I saw him from the window!' he said. 'All mangy and bloody and curiously singed.' 'Who?' I said. '*Makepeace,*' he yelled at me, '*a bloke I work with.*'

Well. I looked out of the window, and there was nobody there. So I told him to get some sleep, but then he did a very curious thing. (I can hardly write this I am so agitated.) He flung up the window and shouted, as if to the empty night sky, a great metaphysical question. '*Makepeace,*' he demanded, '*where is your copy?*'

Such an extraordinary, compelling, sad, and almost beautiful thing to say. Where indeed is *anybody's* copy?

Tim's nocturnal sighting of Makepeace was unremarkable, of course, until you realize that his lifeless corpse had been discovered, earlier that day (Wednesday), in the remains of the shed fire in Angela Farmer's garden.

'What's this?' said Trent Carmichael suddenly. Up to now, his poking through the ruins had been pretty half-hearted and pettish. Not surprisingly, the great detective was a bit cross, having come hotfoot from London in dismal weather on a consultative mercy dash, only to discover that Angela had unilaterally sent her troublesome journalist away straight after breakfast, apparently with a full apology and a small packet of cheese-and-pickle sandwiches. Investigating a burned-out Devonian shed in the presence of that little snot-nose Gordon Clarke was hardly an adequate compensation for this disappointment, and Carmichael was not a man to demonstrate grace under pressure.

'What's what?' replied Angela distractedly. She felt glum. Holding Gordon's hand and suddenly squeezing it, she had just noticed the melted remains of her old wind-up gramophone and was feeling the prickling at the back of her nose which normally (though not very often) presaged the onset of tears. Carmichael pointed to something sticking up out of the ashes. 'Well, to be honest, my dear, it looks like – well, it looks like a human hand.'

It was true. They all stared. Angela was so surprised she forgot to tell him off for calling her 'my dear'. From amid the mess of blackened timbers, charred pots and smouldering paper, a curled, blackened, human hand reached out, the index finger extended, and the whole thing rocked slightly, rather as though its owner were saying 'Over here!' or trying to beckon a waiter.

'Oh God, that's terrible,' said Gordon, in a very small voice.

'Who is it?' whispered Carmichael. He took the opportunity to steal a comforting arm around Angela's shoulders, but impatiently she shook it off.

'For God's sake,' she bawled, 'are you telling me I have a barbecued stiff in my shed? Is this some kind of a joke?'

Nobody had the stomach to see what else was underneath, but Gordon recognized the remains of his dad's hatchet lying nearby, and also Makepeace's bag of bicycle bits (lamps, pump, chain and padlock, all buckled from the heat), so it was pretty obvious whose hand was sticking out here, arrested for all eternity in the futile act of trying to order an extra round of poppadoms. Poor Makepeace. The man who was never wrong. A lot of people, when they heard the news of his passing, would sigh and hang their heads, and remember him. And they would think, 'Thank heaven I'm never going to be bullied by that bloody little know-all again.'

'What I don't understand,' said Carmichael, turning to Angela, 'is how you didn't see or hear anything. Isn't that your bedroom immediately above here? Wouldn't you notice that there was a fire burning? Wouldn't you hear the crackles, see the lights, feel the heat?'

Gordon frowned and looked at Angela. He hated to admit it, but Carmichael had a point. Angela was a light sleeper; plus she had a stranger locked up in the house; plus she was blushing heavily now, in a manner he'd never seen before.

For herself, Angela found it hard to answer this question with any degree of honesty, especially as her own internal shed-burning – complete with crackles, lights and licky hot flames – was merely dormant, and honestly might flare up again at any moment if she gave a single thought to the night's events.

'I don't want the cops involved,' she snapped.

'OK.'

There was a pause. They all looked around. The hand waved; 'Excuse me –'

'Any reason?' asked Carmichael casually, as though it didn't really matter.

'Yep.' She pulled her jacket around her shoulders, and gave a brave smile to Gordon. She was wondering whether to tell him she had taken Osborne as a willing sex slave and temporarily concealed him in the garage with a stack of cup cakes and the bunny for company. But possibly, on second thoughts, he was a bit too young to understand.

'Right,' said Carmichael. 'I mean, you don't have to tell me, if you don't want to.'

'You're dead right I don't.' Angela sniffed, and lit a cigarette.

'So what do you want me to do?' he exploded. 'What do you want me to *detect*? After all, we know who's under there. Also, we assume it was an accident –'

'Of course it was.'

'So I'm just not quite sure where my expertise comes in.'

They all looked at the hand. It seemed to be beckoning, in a polite sort of gesture, as if to say, 'Sorry to be a nuisance, but I wonder, could I have a word?'

'What would Inspector Greenfinger do?' asked Gordon, tearing his gaze away.

'He'd sit down for a minute indoors, if he had any sense,' said Angela.

'Just right,' said Carmichael. 'He would say, "Well, Pete" – Pete is his sidekick, but you knew that – "Well, Pete, I don't think that fellow is going anywhere!" and surge indoors for a cup of hot, strong camomile tea.'

'Swell,' said Angela.

They turned to go inside. The hand could wait. Carmichael, eager to change the subject, started telling them the plot of his next novel, in which the victim was found with a big old-fashioned watering-can forced down over his head. They chuckled appreciatively. 'He yells for help through the spout, but no one hears him,' he added proudly. 'In fact, he is only found eventually when someone inadvertently trips over the handle.'

They all laughed and speeded up, heading gratefully for the back door. What a ghastly way to spend an afternoon. Thank goodness it was over.

And meanwhile the blackened hand still signalled from the debris. 'Er, I don't suppose you could hold on a minute?' it said. 'I just feel sure there is something you haven't taken into account. If you could just – Hello? Excuse me –'

But they had gone.

The thing about Lillian's clever choice of disguise – as travelling fluffy-bunny salesperson – was that it rather defeated her intention. In some vague indefinable way (but something to do with a tall, striking, baby-blonde woman trailing soft toys about in broad daylight) it just didn't help her to blend into the surrounding landscape. People pointed her out; small children scoffed and jeered; and Gordon, first thing in the morning, brought up an ironical extra little breakfast tray with just a lettuce leaf on it. But if she wanted to change her cover story to something else, it was a bit late now. And besides, if she was honest, she rather liked the bunny she'd bought at the shops. He was woolly and earnest-looking, and, like all the best soft toys, he was a very good listener. Certainly he was a comfort in this ghastly unnecessary mess she had got herself into. He was her only ally. For if Michelle and Makepeace had contrived to get rid of Osborne (she was still sure of this), and if Angela Farmer and the Dunquenchin team had lent their support – well, that only left the soft toy she could trust.

But she had dropped the bunny when she saw Tim in the High Street; and now, to cap it all, she'd been robbed. Somebody had taken the letters. Those nutsy letters Michelle had written, about wanting to stake out Osborne and do horrid things to his nipples – they had been stolen from her room by somebody during the day, when she was out fruitlessly casing the Farmer house. All in all, it was no wonder she felt pretty insecure. No sign of Osborne any more; no friendly furry helpmeet with long floppy ears; and when she got back to her room in the evening, not only were the letters gone, but there was a little drop of blood on the carpet and the room was permeated by the curious and unpleasant odour of singed hair. On top of which, an insane missive was attached to her pillow. In a mad scrawl it said: 'Knowledge is Power, and you know *nothing*.'

The only person to have a fairly good day was Osborne. No sane person would choose to be cooped up in a dark, empty, paraffin-smelling garage while a legendary thriller-writer sleuths for clues twenty yards away; but on the other hand, Osborne was not slow to appreciate the chance of forty winks. Angela's sudden and virulent arrival in his life had been cataclysmic, and the result was that a little lie-down was called for. 'I'll come get you as soon as I can,' she promised as she lowered the up-and-over door, sealing out the natural light; but inwardly he begged her not to rush. He felt he had been wrenched, pushed, dragged, drawn and wrung; he felt like a weed that has forced its way through concrete. The sight of the cup cakes made him feel sick.

Most of the day he snoozed, intermittently waking up to switch on his torch and read a few more pages from Trent Carmichael's nasty *S is for ... Secateurs!* before snuggling down in a nest of old blankets, peeling a cup cake, and surrendering himself to the far from unpleasant feeling that, at present, there was precisely nothing he could do. This was true, of course. If *Come Into the Garden* had folded, there was nothing he could do. And if Makepeace had been sizzled to a crisp in the shed fire (as Angela popped in to tell him during the afternoon), well, there wasn't much he could do about that either. Of course he felt sorry for the little chap, but it was curiously difficult to regret his passing, or even fully to believe in it. During one of his many snoozes, he hallucinated that Makepeace was being buried, yet kept insisting on sitting up in the coffin. 'You're dead,' people told him. 'I am *not*,' he protested. 'Come on, lie down.' 'I *won't*.'

Lucky that Osborne appreciated this chance to loll about; lucky that he believed in 'sleep debt' the way other people believed in overdrafts. In fact, he thought of his daily ten hours of nod in precisely the same balance-sheet terms: that if you draw out you must pay in; and that when you overdraw consistently, ultimately you receive a nasty letter threatening to revoke your credit facilities until further notice. So he stretched, yawned, snuggled down with his eyes closed, and let his thoughts wander across the border into Bo-Bo Land. The rabbit stirred, and unconsciously he scratched its ears. For Osborne, sleep was the constant state, the default mode to which he always returned when his attention was not demanded elsewhere. Everyday life might extend distractions to pull him out of the sack, but the moment it relaxed its grip, he sank back gladly into catalepsy. Sometimes it seemed to him that even if he slept till the millennium, he would simply never catch up. Osborne's sleep debt was evidently of prodigious proportions, somewhere along the lines of the Public Sector Borrowing Requirement.

Turning over to get more comfortable, he thought vaguely about *S is for ... Secateurs!* and wondered what everyone saw in it. The story concerned a precocious pubescent girl, physically unattractive but jailbait none the less, who blackmailed two older men after involving them in the dismemberment and disposal of a body. It seemed that, partly crazed by a youthful perusal of the works of Sigmund Freud, this West Country Lolita had killed her father over a misunderstanding at the allotments, when at the fervid height of her teenage sexual alertness she overheard him tempting a schoolfriend with a giant marrow. 'Do you see how it's grown?' he said in all innocence. 'Tell you what, I'll treat you to a bit later, if you're interested.' It was a tragic choice of words – especially for a man whose psychotic daughter not only harboured a burgeoning Electra complex, but whose favourite job was sharpening the blades of the hedge clipper.

Osborne squirmed slightly at the memory. He pictured the large garden in *S is for ... Secateurs!*, extraordinarily similar to Angela's, in which the burials took place. It disappointed him that Carmichael had modelled the topography so closely on a real locale; what a shame it was when novelists didn't bother to make things up. In the story, the garden had the same dark poplar trees, the same ancient mulberry, the pergola, and (of course) the magnificent shed. It occurred to him suddenly that the sinister author picture he had seen on the back of *Murder, Shear Murder* actually showed the out-of-focus shape of Angela's shed in the background. Ho hum. Another instance of lack of imagination.

But it occurred to him also, as his mind started its slow, struggling ascent out of the pit of slumber, that a line from one of the G. Clarke letters didn't really make sense. 'I haven't even *met* Trent Carmichael ... ' it said. There was something wrong with that. What, though? He switched on his torch, and got the letter out of his pocket: 'I haven't even *met* Trent Carmichael.' He scratched his head. Well, of course the real G. Clarke *did* know Carmichael, but that wasn't the point. It was that – oh yes, good heavens, this letter had been written *before the Carmichael piece appeared in the magazine*. He sat up so quickly that he bumped his head on a fire extinguisher. 'Bugger,' he said, but it was only a reflex.

This Carmichael reference was significant. How could somebody respond to a piece that wasn't yet in print – to a piece, in fact, that had never been published at all, because the magazine had closed down in the week it was due to appear? There was only one person who knew he had written it: Michelle. He gasped as he considered the implications. It was Michelle who wanted him to rummage in her shed. It was Michelle who wanted to dress up in a négligé and gardening gloves and flip-flops. Which was why, when the garage door flipped momentarily open, and a small figure scurried in wearing a loose frock and carrying a pitchfork, he yelled, above the boom of the closing door, 'Michelle! Oh God, you've come to get me!'

'You're wrong there, as usual,' said a familiar voice. And suddenly the garage reeked of burning hair.

12

Up in the office at Dunquenchin, Gordon was having a breakthrough. He might have shouted 'Eureka!' if his classical education had been better; as it was, he shouted 'Dad!' Twelve months of terribly advanced electronic remote-contact wizardry with teams of Californian graphics experts, combined with neurological analysis of such amazing complexity and sophistication that quite honestly you or I would never understand it – *even (ahem) if it could be described in words* – had finally culminated in that virtual reality program he had called, provisionally, *Phototropism.*

It was Thursday morning, and breakfast was finished. It seemed the perfect opportunity for a test run. Hearing the footsteps of his dad coming up the stairs, Gordon strapped a custom-built Fly-Mo unit to his bonce (or that's what it looked like), thrust his hand into a wired-up glove, adjusted quickly to the intense consuming dark, and for the very first time surrendered himself to the entirety of the finished game. Though he was a pioneer, he felt safe and confident. Earlier, his dad had commented kindly, 'You need taking out of yourself, son'; and Gordon had promptly decided that a 'proto-photo-trip' was precisely the thing required. In theory, the program would trigger receptors in his brain to convince him – little by little, and depending on the level of skill – that his entire body was growing and reaching out like a plant in sunlight. It would take him out of himself, exactly.

What Gordon seemed to have seriously miscalculated, however, was the rate of acceleration. As it now transpired, being taken out of yourself from nought to infinity in fifteen seconds is pretty terrifying, and slightly more than the normal human constitution can withstand. From the evidence of his earlier partial test runs, Gordon had expected a slow but perceptible unfurling sensation, like an exquisite lily opening gracefully on the surface of a tranquil Japanese pond: starting with warm earlobes and a tingling sensation under the skin, it would then progress to something delicate around the eyelids. Instead, however, as his whole body instantly convulsed and whiplashed in his chair, the main sensations were of being violently drawn, wrung, pushed, dragged and wrenched. It was horrific. He screamed as his fingers spread and stretched, creaking and splitting, as his arms and legs tugged fiercely at their sockets, as even his hair yanked painfully at his head.

The large Victorian bedroom he could see around him (a virtual reality black-and-white 3D drawing, based on the Tenniel illustrations from *Alice)* shrank in on him, *foop!*, like that; in two seconds flat, Gordon had his foot up the chimney, and his arm out of the window, and was just about to swell up fatally against the ceiling when – *beep!*, the machine apparently switched itself off. As the picture dimmed and Gordon felt himself dwindle to normal size, he noticed a little tray of cakes marked EAT ME, which were presumably part of his Californian designer's homage to Lewis Carroll. Even in the throes of his peculiar ecstasy, and even at only nineteen years old, Gordon's detumescent brain thought, Hang on, that's a bit suggestive, I'd better work on that.

He removed the lawn-mower helmet in a state of utter shock and disbelief. His head was hot, his eyes saw patterns in the air and his ears throbbed. When he tried to speak (just to exclaim 'Lumme'), he vomited and started sobbing. No wonder he was upset: if this was its usual physiological effect, *Phototropism* obviously had a very limited future in the penny arcades. Gordon's proto-photo-trip had lasted exactly six seconds and had taken about ten years off his life. If his dad had not burst into the room and taken the initiative of unplugging the machine, he might shortly have gone insane.

'Do you want to talk about it?' his dad said later, when Gordon had stopped shaking and was sipping from a large mug of hot sugared tea.

'I don't think I can.'

'Sure you can. What did it feel like? Was it anything like growing?'

Gordon yowled, nodded and suppressed a snivel.

'Why do I get the impression that growing isn't a pleasant experience?' Gordon's dad said warmly, to no one in particular, and then hugged his son again. 'What else is worrying you, eh? Tell your old dad. What's been going on in that brilliant loaf of yours? I suppose it's that *hand*?' (His tone suggested the hand was to blame, as if to say, 'Just wait till I catch that hand, I'll show it the back of my – er, hand.')

But at the mention of the hand, Gordon, usually such an equable lad, let go of everything he'd been bottling up, with an explosive outburst rather like an accident in a compressed-air factory.

'But he's *dead*, Dad,' he yelled, 'that Makepeace is. Died in the fire on Tuesday night. Lying there all charred and it's my fault, because I got scared of him and you locked him in and I feel so guilty now –'

'But hang on,' his dad interrupted, 'I'm sure he was in here yesterday again. I –'

'No, he's *dead*. Definitely. I saw the *hand*, and now I'm worried because Angela let the other one go, and that creep

Trent Carmichael is here, and I know there's something horrible going on between him and Margaret, always has been, something really nasty, and Margaret's a cow, Dad, she's really horrible to that ex-boyfriend, and he's looking really *worried*, and now my *program* doesn't work properly –'

'Could anyone have tampered with it?'

'What? No. I mean, well yes, but who would? Anyway, that's not all. Now I've sacked a lot of innocent people I don't even know, and what else, right, the tall woman in the pink coat keeps trying to make friends with me on the landing by talking baby talk as though I were *three – years – old!*'

He paused. He wiped a tear. There was no more.

'You're right about Margaret, you know,' said his dad after a bit. 'My own brother's daughter, God rest him, but such a rotten cow that you can hardly credit it. She had a great pile of notes on that boyfriend, you know. Loads of it. Brought it with her. Tapes as well, photos, samples of shopping lists, everything. She's writing a book.'

'No. What, on Tim? What's he done?'

'Just been himself, that's all. But as far as Margaret's concerned, he's a fruitcake. All that guff about those daffodil bulbs. You know.'

'Poor bloke, that's awful. What a *cow*.'

'Yes. Anyway, I found it this morning when I was making her bed, so I took it straight round to his room, poor bloke, and said take a butcher's at this.'

Gordon gasped. 'You didn't.'

'Why not?'

'No, I mean, it's brilliant. I think that's brilliant, Dad. But you realize she'll go berserk?'

'I don't care.'

'No?'

'No.'

Gordon dropped his voice, as if to raise something delicate.

'So she hasn't, sort of, *got* anything on you? No secrets, you know, no nasty buried stuff?'

'Of course not.'

Gordon was relieved. 'It's just she always gives the impression she knows something to your disadvantage.'

'I know. But that's because she's a *cow*.'

'Right.'

'Which she is.'

'Absolutely.'

'What a *cow*!' exclaimed Tim.

Ten minutes ago he had been lying in bed, miserable, listening with distant interest to a rather combative programme on Radio 4 called *Face the Facts*, and worrying heavily about nothing whatsoever. The things he faced were not facts, but they loomed larger than reality, and that was the trouble. This morning he had been particularly preoccupied by the vivid mental picture of his next-door neighbour in London, Mrs Lewis, carelessly leaving the front door wide open after feeding Lester. He simply *knew* it was true; he could *see* it, for goodness' sake – open, flapping, people wandering in for a look round, while Mrs Lewis blithely packed her bags and embarked on a fortnight's holiday without a backward glance.

When he tried to suppress this unfounded anxiety, perversely it only grew and stretched in his mind so that by the end it entailed Mrs Lewis (Oh no, was this trustless woman *Welsh?* It explained a lot) absent-mindedly placing a magnifying mirror next to a net curtain, and the low November sun reflecting off it and starting a huge fire, and then Lester rushing frantically into the street and being almost knocked down by a fire engine, which swerved to avoid him and instead ploughed into a bus shelter packed with schoolchildren, exploding with enormous loss of life.

Tim winced miserably and wondered whether to phone his own number, just to check that the line was not 'unobtainable', but he had done this lots of times before, from the office, and knew it didn't prove much. In the old days, when he and Margaret lived together, they would sometimes come out of the tube station and, walking home, address his fears in sequential order, with Margaret's natural sarcasm reined in as tightly as it would go. 'Phew, the *neighbourhood is* still here,' Tim would say, amazed, as they emerged in the daylight. 'All right so far, then,' said Margaret. They turned a corner. 'Wow, our *road* is still here,' said Tim. 'A very good sign,' she agreed. They held their breath until the trees cleared to reveal in the distance their own abode still standing, and not a blackened shell surrounded by ambulances. 'The *house is* still there. Look, the *house.*' 'Hallelujah.' They moved closer, not running, but walking more urgently. 'And thank God, I don't believe it, I think the *flat's* still there!' 'Oh yes,' said Margaret. 'It's a miracle.'

But Tim now had an additional worry, and a pleasingly circular one at that. Possibly he was really bonkers – and anxiety about being bonkers was the first sign that you were mad. Certainly Margaret's purse-lipped, arms-folded, tut-tut attitude to his repeated sightings of work colleagues in Honiton would suggest that she thought he was barking, but was too polite to say. Last night he had actually seen *Osborne*, by the way, which brought the running total to four. Looking out of the window, he thought he saw the 'Me and My Shed' man being ferried, trussed up, through the quiet streets of Honiton on the front of a push-bike pedalled by a small, black, hairy figure in a frock with a trident, like Britannia – possibly a child, or possibly a clever, cycling, costumed chimp escaped from a patriotic circus. Tim had accepted it, at the time. Now it seemed pretty sick.

The radio didn't help, this *Face the Facts* stuff, especially since the reporter seemed so certain of everything. Not a flicker of doubt was present in his mind. 'So we confronted Mr Chimneypot at his new premises in Gloucester Road,' he announced. The soundtrack cut from the studio to the outdoor swish of passing traffic, the panting huff-puff of the reporter chasing someone up to their front door and sticking his foot in it. 'What about your investors, Mr Chimneypot? Is Chimneypot your real name? Are there any little Chimneypots? Can you tell us anything about Kiss Me Quick PLC –'

'Why don't they leave him alone?' thought Tim, as he switched it off. 'In any case, where do they get the moral energy?' But then Margaret's uncle knocked on his own door and offered him this great pile of stuff about how he was a case-book nutcase; and amazingly (paradoxically, you might call it), ten minutes later he wasn't mad any more. Except, of course, in the sense of absolutely hopping. 'What a rotten *cow*,' he exclaimed again, leaping out of bed, and pulling on some clothes. He switched the radio back on. 'That was *Face the Facts*,' said the announcer. Yes, thought Tim, it certainly was.

'I'm going to kill her,' he said. 'Look, she's got my Post-it stickers and everything. She's set me up.' He read the latest notes again, scanning for the bits that annoyed him most – 'personality implodes ... inevitable breakdown ... nudge him off into the abyss ... traumatized by displays of sexuality ... hates the sight of cream' – and let out a very uncharacteristic bellow of rage. 'WOOOOORH!' he went, feeling surprisingly good about it. 'WOOOOORH!' He had come down here to this godforsaken town to find the bastard who'd taken his job away, and been sidetracked into acting the invalid, just because of that *cow* Margaret. 'WOORH!' he went (slightly shorter this time). He didn't even know what he was doing in this bloody B&B. 'WORH!' he went, kicking some files.

He felt quite exhausted. He needed to sit down. And the

very last 'WRH' he made – just before Gordon tapped on the door and came in, and they somehow got on to the subject of who'd bought *Come Into the Garden* – was actually quite quiet.

'The thing you've got to remember about Margaret,' said Trent Carmichael to Michelle, as they watched her walk past their coffee-shop window, smiling privately to herself about something, 'is that she is an absolute *cow*.'

Michelle nodded. She knew the type.

'I mean it. Whatever you do,' he warned her, showing his teeth, 'don't tell her anything personal.'

'I won't.' Michelle thought about it. 'You mean the rubberized gardening-glove fetish sort of thing?'

'Exactly. She'd make something of it.'

'I understand. She resembles that sinister patricidal girl in *S is for ... Secateurs!*, then?'

'Yes. In fact you might say she's the very model.'

They continued to stare out of the window, until Michelle broke the silence.

'She knows something about *you*, does she?'

'Alas, yes.'

'Pillow talk, was it?'

'Sadly, you're right.'

Michelle stiffened. She hated the thought of sharing Trent with another woman, especially a *cow* like Margaret.

'Actually, my little dung beetle (if I may),' Trent continued, 'it does occur to me that you still haven't told *me* anything personal, either, yet, except that you've got a mother you have to phone twice a day who loves my books almost to the point of obsession, and who can't wait to meet me.'

He put a hand on her thigh. It thrilled her.

'Haven't I?' she said, attempting an airy manner, but feeling her face redden.

'No.'

'Mm.' He moved his hand. He was awfully good at this.

'I've guessed a lot, though. I can't help looking for clues, you know, being a crime writer. I think I've, you know, ratiocinated quite a lot about you.'

'Such as?'

'Well, you are clever, obviously. But you're pale, you stay indoors a lot, and you don't have a boyfriend, and you do your nails, but not very well.' He smiled apologetically. She smiled back, allowed him to continue.

'Now, your clothes are a bit old-fashioned, and you obviously don't know how to communicate with people, and you have a devotional air and know about gardening, and you've got this big gap in your life going back, ooh, fifteen years.'

'So?'

'So I reckon you're a lapsed nun.'

Michelle said nothing. She felt like laughing, but thought it would be rude.

'I'm right, aren't I?' said Trent.

She took a long, thoughtful drink of coffee.

'Well, put it this way,' she said, at last. 'You're not exactly wrong.'

She looked out of the window and smiled to herself. Two days ago she'd been in the office, doing usual Tuesday things. A mere forty-eight hours later she was in a Devon teashop with a famous lover with sympathetic kinky ideas, a plate of free cream buns, and a mysterious past involving wimples. What did she usually do at 11 a.m. on a Thursday morning? Good heavens, she'd forgotten. She'd almost forgotten about Osborne, too; but not quite.

'Trent, you know, I'm a twinge angry with you, my darling Green Thumb (if I may). You still haven't told me what happened yesterday, at your friend Angela's. Did you find out what was wrong with this – who was it, um, I forget – this shed journalist? Storm in a teacup, was it? I don't suppose he had a hatchet, did he? Just some silly mistake.'

'Well, actually, no.' Carmichael looked around, and moved his chair closer to hers. 'If you can keep a secret,' he virtually whispered. 'Actually, he's dead. The shed burned down with him – and the hatchet – inside it. Dreadful business.'

Michelle went white. Dead? Her lovely Osborne? Dead? Dead, in a shed?

'Where is this place? I want to see it,' she cried, getting up suddenly and knocking over a trolley of cakes.

Carmichael stared at her with surprise and admiration. This woman was a real dark horse.

'It's down the lane from the guesthouse,' he said. 'Past the Chimneypot Garden Centre. You can't miss it, it's got a burned-out shed in the garden.'

Angela had been mortified to find Osborne gone. Not only had he scarpered without saying goodbye, he had also taken the blankets, the cakes, the book and the rabbit. Jesus, men were such lousy scumbags. She slung an empty gin bottle into the rubbish, where it clanked against all the other bottles she'd emptied since yesterday. Vodka, Bailey's, sangria, Tizer, Worcester sauce – it had been a very long night, and she had invented some deeply unusual cocktails. And now she was giddily propping herself up at the kitchen window, all the weight on her forearms, frowning against a swirling mental fog, and barking down the phone to Gordon ('Ah, a *proto*-scumbag,' she thought, viciously), who had innocently rung her, to ask to come round.

'Jesus' sakes, Gordon, sure she's a *cow*.' Staggering, she

looked around for a stool to sit on, but there wasn't one, so she just collapsed on the kitchen vinyl, pulling the phone down on top of her with a crash. 'You still there? OK. No, I'm fine. But don't sound so shocked about whatsername, yeah, Margaret. I've told you a million times she's a cow. I wouldn't trust her further than I can throw my own pancreas.'

Just next to her face on the floor she noticed a small drip of golden liquid (the last of the whisky, perhaps?) and realized that if she moved her body a couple of inches to the left, she could probably lick it.

She turned her attention to Gordon. 'A cow is what she always was, Gordon baby. Barney left me because of her, I know it.' Actually, she'd never thought of this before, but she was free-associating, and it sounded like sense. 'Yeah, sure. I always knew it. Something they did together. Sometimes I've even wondered whether that *S is for ... Secateurs!* was all about her and Barney and Trent. All that spooky burial stuff, you know.'

The proto-scumbag asked to come round. She said, 'Sure'. He needed advice. He said he'd just discovered that the B&B was crawling with disaffected staff from *Come Into the Garden*, one of whom was the ex-boyfriend of Margaret.

'Small world,' said Angela bitterly, not very interested in *Come Into the Garden* any more. 'Sure, come.' She hung up the phone, and added glumly, 'I've got nobody else here.'

She lay on her back. Scumbags, she thought. Manderley, what a joke. She made a decision and licked up the drip of whisky. It had some dirt in it, but it was OK. Then, with her arms folded across her chest and her eyes tightly closed, she surrendered herself to the familiar round-and-round out-of-body sensation she fondly called the helicopters, only this time it made her think of Wagner's 'Ride of the Valkyries', she didn't know why.

Tim and Gordon walked along together to Angela's house.

'She's a *cow*,' muttered Tim.

'You're right,' said Gordon.

'I'm glad we burned it.'

'Me too.'

Tim kicked a stone.

'I still can't believe you're the bastard who's closed down the mag.'

'Sorry.'

'I mean, it meant such a lot to me.'

'I know.'

'It was the thing I could count on, you know. A sort of shelter. I feel really exposed without it. I'm not sure I can survive in the outside world. I'm too weedy.'

'But you can survive without Margaret?'

'That's true. She's a cow.'

'You're right.'

'I'm quite excited about meeting Angela Farmer. I'm a fan.'

'Oh, she's terrific, you'll love her.'

It was only when they arrived at the gate that they heard a woman scream, from the vicinity of the burned-out shed. It was Michelle. She was standing in the ashes, holding a blackened hand (somebody else's) up to her face and shrieking. But as they raced towards her, they realized she was shrieking with hysterical laughter, not fear. 'It's not a real one,' she yelled to them, more loudly than was necessary, as they reached her, panting. She seemed exhilarated by relief. Tim was confused, he had never seen her so animated. 'I've seen hundreds of these. Look, it's just latex or something. My mother buys them in job lots. She's obsessed with *S is for ... Secateurs!* and the others; always trying to re-create great moments from it.'

They all looked at the hand.

'So Makepeace isn't dead, then?' gasped Gordon.

'Makepeace?' said Tim and Michelle, with a single voice.

'But what was a trick severed hand doing in Angela's shed?' asked Gordon, puzzled. 'It wasn't there before.'

Michelle shrugged. Now Trent Carmichael had appeared at the gate, as well as Gordon's dad and, separately, Lillian. What the hell was Lillian doing here? 'Hi, Lillian,' said Tim, whom nothing surprised any more. 'I thought it was you I saw. Everybody's here, then. I even saw Osborne last night. Although, come to think of it, he didn't look too happy in his role as the spoils of Britannia.'

But his voice faded on the air, and everyone looked at Michelle. Somehow it seemed like a moment of truth. The hand wanted to tell them something! As they all stood still in Angela's garden, they surveyed the scene as though they had never seen it before (to be fair, some of them hadn't), and tried to comprehend the full meaning of it all. Here, beside the shed, was the small area of recently dug earth where Makepeace had uncovered the hand. All around them, the autumnal garden held its breath, keeping its secrets, the very image of life suspended. Wordlessly they were gathering at the shed, to see the hand. It was a moment of deadly solemnity.

Angela, with her gumboots on the wrong feet, staggered across the lawn to join them.

'I expect you're wondering why I've asked you all here,' she said, beaming. And then vomited copiously on Trent Carmichael's shoes.

13

Although Osborne still could not imagine why the rabbit had been brought along, he was extremely glad of the company, especially now that Makepeace had gone off and left him shackled in a Lumberland Alpine Resteezy in a windy, deserted garden centre just two hundred yards from Dunquenchin. He stroked the rabbit and, in the absence of anything more suitable, fed it a cake wrapper and some wood shavings, which it appeared to enjoy thoroughly. Being locked in confined spaces was becoming second nature to him, he reflected. Were he ever to get out of Honiton alive, he would hereafter only accept house-sitting jobs which offered smallish airing cupboards, or coal bunkers, or larders, where he could sit in the dark with a pile of junk food wondering vaguely whether someone would come along at any minute and kill him.

Did Makepeace intend to kill him? Surely not. Just because he had assumed the *alter ego of* Loony Gordon, complete with négligé and flip-flops, didn't mean he was bound by destiny to perpetrate violence. Just because he had furtively experimented with *Phototropism* for dangerously lengthy periods, and it had turned the balance of his mind so that he honestly no longer had any conception of his actual size – all this did not mean he must behave like King Kong, Gog, Magog and Godzilla rolled into one. And just because he was all sooty and singed and his hair was still smouldering didn't mean he must automatically assume all the other savage attributes of the Wild Man of Borneo.

Last week, for heaven's sake, this small, long-haired intellectual contortionist had written a deliberately incomprehensible thousand-word review for *The Times Literary Supplement* on the subject of Norwegian poetry – quoting much of it in the original language, moreover, with its o's crossed out, and everything. From such spectacular brainbox ostentation to a state of primal savagery it was surely impossible to plummet in a seven-day period, however eventful or surprising those seven days might somehow conspire to be.

Makepeace was certainly a little unbalanced, however. Even Osborne was obliged to concede it. 'Seen *these* before, you tiny *minuscule* person?' Makepeace had yelled at Osborne overexcitedly, chucking a fat file of papers at his recumbent friend, on their first reunion in Angela Farmer's pitch-dark garage. 'They come from – *Dunquenchin!*' In the ghostly illumination shed by Osborne's feeble torch beam, these papers were revealed to be more – possibly hundreds more – letters from G. Clarke to the author of 'Me and My Shed', half of them dwelling quite gratuitously on what a frightful and appalling writer he was, the others filled with drooling fantasy about rubbing green liquid lawn-feed into his skin, or binding his body in a length of half-inch garden hose before imaginatively employing his hardened willy in the greenhouse as a sort of improvised dibber.

As before, Osborne saw straight to the essence of these letters, and took the critical ones to heart.

'Oh look, oh that's not fair,' he wailed, time after time, shuffling the papers for the worst bits and frowning at the smarts of unfair accusation. In the blackness of the garage, his little torch beam skidded madly around the walls and ceiling, as he gesticulated his misery and hurt. 'Oh, but my Val Doonican piece was one of my *best*. Oh. Oh, this is vicious, really. And I *did* mention the knitwear. I even mentioned bright elusive butterflies. These are very unfair, Makepeace. I hope you didn't read them?'

Makepeace made no reply.

Osborne read some more. 'Blah blah ... garden hose ... lily-white skin ... blah blah ... dibber ... blah blah ... hang on, what was that dibber bit? Good lord ... blah blah ... Ah! Listen to this, listen. '"I sometimes wonder have you even really been to meet the famous celebrities whose sheds you write about, you make them so uninteresting."' Osborne turned off his torch and put his head in his hands. 'God, that's *so* depressing.'

He felt wretched – and not just because 'famous celebrities' was a tautology, either. How miserable to contemplate Michelle, ostensibly his friend and colleague, composing these poisonous epistles, doubtless at the same time as he was blithely tapping out his inoffensive weekly column in an adjoining room. It was like finding out not only that your mother never loved you, but that in your infancy she also instigated a detrimental whispering campaign ('Smelly feet, pass it on') amongst your family, schoolfriends, teachers and soft toys. For the first time since embarking on this disastrous adventure to the West Country, he seriously wanted to cry.

Meanwhile Makepeace, whose figure he could only faintly discern in the blackness, shuffled with impatience.

'What about the others?' Makepeace urged significantly, in a deep whisper. 'The other letters.'

'How do you mean?' Blindly, Osborne felt around on the floor for more papers.

'The threats, you know. The pitchfork, the dibber. Surely you know by now that *Gordon means every word he writes.*'

Osborne frowned, confused. 'No, it was our chief sub who

wrote these,' he said, his heart so filled with sadness that it welled in his throat and almost choked him. 'Sorry I didn't tell you, but I only just worked it out myself. Can you believe it? She hates me that much.'

There was a menacing laugh from Makepeace, but Osborne was too unhappy to notice. 'You know who I mean? Michelle, in the office. Is she jealous, do you think? Why couldn't she tell me some other way?'

Instead of offering an opinion, however, Makepeace told him to shut up. 'Don't be so ridiculous,' he hissed, in that now wearily familiar ding-ding warning-bell tone of his. 'Gordon wrote these!'

'No, really –'

'*Gordon.*'

'N –' Belatedly Osborne caught the unmissable gist, and quickly reconsidered his position. 'Oh yes, you're right,' he said, promptly.

'Thanks.'

There was silence. Osborne reached for his torch, turned it on, and pretended to fiddle with it aimlessly, while trying to get a partial view of Makepeace. He whistled a tune, waved the torch, cuddled the rabbit and concentrated hard on being somewhere else. After all, what he saw of Makepeace in fractions and spectral glimpses – a gash of vermilion lipstick, for a start – did not encourage him to wish he were here.

'Actually I was worried about you,' he said conversationally. 'People seemed to think you had been in the shed when it burned down.'

'I was.' Makepeace had moved closer. His voice was quite loud.

'Yes, but, well – they also thought, ha ha, you were dead.'

'Which I am, of course. In a manner of speaking.'

Recognizing the need to tread delicately at this juncture, Osborne said merely, 'Oh?'

'I just rose from the ashes, that's all.'

'Nice. Mm. I see.'

'And now I'm G. Clarke of Honiton.'

'Did you say – ? Oh. Well, that's great for you. Great. Congratulations.'

'And I have a destiny.'

'Smashing.'

'Which is why I'm here with you.'

'Oh. I mean, goody.'

There seemed little to say.

'Where did you get the lipstick?'

'At Dunquenchin, of course.'

'Suits you.'

'Thanks. Hey, you can call me Gordon, if you like.'

'I'll try.'

Osborne sighed. He wondered how long he could keep this up. Humouring Makepeace was not his greatest natural talent. And perhaps he shouldn't try so hard, in any case. Because whatever he did, it was obviously simply a matter of time before the little bastard punched him on the nose.

'I don't suppose it struck you,' ventured Makepeace at last, 'how closely I resembled Gordon in the first place?'

'You're right,' said Osborne. 'Yes, I do see what you mean. Absolutely. Although I suppose what did slightly confuse me, why I didn't think you were identical twins separated at birth,' he said, choosing his words carefully, 'was the extraordinary difference in height.'

'Meaning?'

Osborne was glad, now, to be in the pitch dark. He let it out.

'He's a lot taller than you, that's all. You know. Tall.'

At which point, from out of the blackness, Makepeace hit him so hard on the jaw that it knocked him unconscious. And that was that.

So now, next morning, Osborne was alone with the rabbit again, in this draughty shed in a deserted garden centre (winter opening: weekends only). Goodness knows how Makepeace had acquired the strength to shift him, but he'd done it somehow, possibly with the aid of the bike. Rubbing his sore, bruised face, Osborne thought of Angela and sighed. She was such a wonderful person, he was sorry he had let her down. Manderley, oh yes. Last night he dreamed he went to Manderley again. He hoped she hadn't noticed his disappearance; he hoped (with just a smidgen of self-pity) that she would hereafter have a nice life without him. He sniffed. He wanted to be with her. But unfortunately he was tied up at the moment, at the mercy of a short-house know-all transvestite with colossal delusions and a surprisingly effective right hook.

Makepeace, of course, had crept back upstairs in Dunquenchin for a final blast of *Phototropism* before fulfilling his grisly destiny. Luckily all the residents were presently at Angela's (at this precise moment, in fact, all were staring aghast at the noxious pile of sick that had suddenly appeared on Trent Carmichael's footwear), so the B&B was empty. It was true, as Gordon's dad had suggested, that someone had been tampering with the program. Makepeace, whose understanding of advanced computer science was naturally almost as comprehensive as his knowledge of the twenty-six different words for 'under the weather' in Norwegian, had tweaked the acceleration to its maximum after his very first session. None of that gradual, delicate, eyelid lily-pond nonsense for Makepeace. He was a small man in a hurry.

Nothing in Norwegian poetry had prepared him for *Phototropism*. It was a revelation, an epiphany. It caught him up, wrenched him, forced him to grow and reach. Unfortunately it is quite true that people, unlike plants, do not grow unless they are forced to, or unless someone takes an active interest on their behalf. Left to themselves, they stop. So it was arguable that Makepeace deserved the privilege of *Phototropism*, since he was merely compensating for a lifetime as a loveless retard unchallenged by adversity. But alas, it also helped him identify with Gordon, with whom (as we have seen) he was increasingly infatuated. He plugged in, switched on and screeched outwards like the winds of hell until his body filled the universe.

At Angela's, Michelle was studying the hand and getting impatient. Unlike Trent Carmichael, she was extremely good at deduction, and in fifteen minutes of urgent questioning had pieced together enough information to know that Osborne had disappeared; that Makepeace, previously feared dead, had probably abducted him; and that a mysterious nameless rabbit was also somehow crucially involved. Moreover, as an expert on *S is for ... Secateurs!* (having discussed its plot with her mother on many macabre occasions), she had quickly deduced that this fake hand had been buried in the garden ten years ago by Trent and Barney (precisely in the manner of the two adult male conspirators in the book) in the misguided belief that it belonged to the corpse of Margaret's father.

Since Trent seemed unable to grasp this point for himself, she took him aside and explained it to him.

'You see, if it had been a real hand, it would have decomposed.'

'I know that.'

'And it's not a real hand.' She paused. 'So it didn't.'

'All right, OK,' he conceded miserably.

'So why do I detect a twinge of reluctance to accept it?' she said. She was slightly irritated. For someone who had just heard the happy news that he took no part in a terrible long-ago patricidal carve-up – or more precisely, that no terrible long-ago patricidal carve-up had taken place at all – he seemed less than properly relieved.

'It's just that all these years –' He broke off.

All these years what? thought Michelle, her heart suddenly jerking and flipping in her chest like a yo-yo doing loop-the-loop. All these years, you have depended on the idea that your soul was smeared with guilt? I do love you, she thought, her yo-yo melting behind her ribs. You are so wonderfully *twisted*.

'All these years what?' she encouraged him gently.

Trent Carmichael screwed up his face as though about to spit. 'It's just that all these years that *cow* has been making a fool of me.'

Meanwhile, in the bathroom, Angela's eyes, ears, nose and throat were reacquainting themselves with the cocktails and packet-snacks of the previous night, while Gordon stood manfully beside her with a towel and a bottle of water, humming it's-all-right-I'm-not-looking tunes from *Showboat* and being careful not to mention undercooked eggs; and Lillian, who had been forced to realize that her cherished conspiracy theory against Osborne was precisely wrong in every respect, was making a private phone call from the hall. We will listen in on this conversation, but a word of warning is first required: under the strain of recent developments – not least the drama of Angela's unexpected projectile vomiting – Lillian's baby-talk had deepened so profoundly that it now scarcely qualified as language at all.

'Bunny? Oh, hey-wo bunny, issmeegen bunny.' [*Greetings Bunny, it's me again, also called Bunny.*]

She waited while Mister Bunny yelled, 'Where are you, what's going on?' and simply took no notice. Being in Honiton on the trail of a missing 'Me and My Shed' columnist was an impossible answer to frame within the regressive vocabulary available.

'How Dexie doin, poor ted-babe?' [*How fares Dexter, the sick little bear?*]

'So sorry, bunny, not home. But soon as poss.' [*Full of regrets not to be home yet, all will be revealed in the fullness of time.*]

'Mishu.' [*More regrets.*]

'Oops, money don. So spensive. [*We are about to run out of time; the rate is high.*]

'Bwye!' [*Bye!*]

'Tiss, tiss.' [Kiss *kiss.*]

Only when she replaced the receiver did she notice Gordon's dad watching her from the kitchen door, his face contorted in a grimace of pain.

'Wassamat – I mean, what's the matter?'

Gordon's dad came towards her and put a sympathetic hand on her arm.

'I'm sorry if this seems rude,' he said, 'but were you really talking to somebody? Or just pretending?'

Lillian blushed, and picked at the fluff on her sleeve.

'Does it matter?' she said at last.

'Not to me, no. But I ought to warn you: do that when my niece Margaret is in earshot, and you'll end up reviewed by Professor Anthony Clare in the *Sunday Times* Books section.'

They walked through the kitchen and outside into the garden again. A wind was rocking the trees, blowing ashes and leaves in swirls and loops, making Lillian feel strange and light-headed. Tim had just told her that Gordon was the proprietor who'd sacked her, but she couldn't feel angry about it; she could never dislike this nice man, Gordon's dad. *Come Into the Garden* was another world. Let Clement take her standard lamp if he wanted to: what did she care? If anyone had offered her a lumpy cup-soup with croûtons at this moment, she would have rejected it utterly, waved it away, as an unwelcome reminder of Angela's vomit, nothing more.

'I don't think I've met Margaret,' she said. 'Is she the one everyone says is a cow?'

'That's right. She was writing a book about Tim – your colleague, yes? – but we burned the notes. He seems suddenly a great deal happier now.'

'Tim never mentioned Margaret at the office, you know.'

'Not even when they split up?'

'No. But then we didn't talk about our private lives. I didn't know Michelle had a boyfriend. I just knew she wrote mad letters to Osborne. And I suppose, now I come to think of it, that personally I never talked about Mister Bunny – sorry, I mean, Jeff. No, hang on, no, not Jeff, what is it?'

'Your husband?'

'Mm. Jack. Jerry. George.'

They surveyed the ruined shed. Neither of them quite knew why they were doing it, or why they'd suddenly gone quiet.

'Why did you call yourself Miss Dexter?'

'I've forgotten.'

'I liked the stuffed bunny-rabbit.'

'Thank you.'

'I sent it a lettuce leaf for breakfast.'

'I know.'

'Are you fond of Osborne?'

'I suppose I must be. But not the way Michelle is. She wants to stick sprigs of rosemary up his nose and use his erect member to make holes in potting compost.'

'You'd never guess, to look at her.'

Lillian laughed.

'Could you fancy a walk into town?' said Gordon's dad, offering his arm. The gesture reminded her of Osborne.

'That would be lovely.'

He opened the gate for her, and they set off down the lane.

'I'm sorry about *Come Into the Garden*. Were you there a very long time?'

'Only fifteen years.'

'It must have been good, then?'

There was a pause.

'No,' she said thoughtfully. 'Not good. Just safe.'

'Who in the name of alimentary tracts are – all – these *people?*' barked Angela, hurling herself on to a soft sofa, her face white and shiny, her hair sticking flat to her head. 'Who in particular is that woman shoving her body at Trent Carmichael and why is she waving an amputated mitt?'

'She's another of my sacked employees,' said Gordon glumly, forgetting that she didn't know this yet.

'What? Are you Digger Enterprises?' gasped Michelle, looking for confirmation to Tim, who nodded. 'Good God.' Stunned, she sat down and wrung her hands – her own, then the fake one, and then all three together.

'So are you from the gardening magazine?' asked Carmichael. 'Not a nun, after all?'

Angela exchanged glances with Gordon and leaned forward. 'I used to play scenes like this when I did Shakespeare,' she whispered. 'They'll be talking about moles on their father's cheek soon.' He smiled. She spoke up. 'Anyone else need to know who anyone else is? Feel free, I mean it. Since we are surely on the verge of clearing up a lot of misunderstandings, we might as well start with present company.' She looked around. 'You, sir!' she pointed at Tim, who jumped. 'Who the hell are you? And Gordon, are you aware that your dad just went down the road with a lady in a pink coat whom nobody knows from Zsa Zsa Gabor?'

'Oh, that was Lillian,' chorused Tim, Michelle and Gordon.

Angela raised her eyes.

'And what does *Lillian* do, when she's at home?'

‘Well, at an educated guess,’ said Michelle, ‘probably not much more than she does at work.’

‘What was the best thing about being a secretary?’ asked Gordon’s dad, as they strolled past Dunquenchin and down towards the Chimneypot nursery on the way to the shops.

‘The best thing about being a secretary?’ she repeated. She blinked, and thought quite hard, but somehow nothing would come.

‘I mean, did you take a pride in it?’

The question was definitely in English, but Lillian still seemed puzzled by it. She stopped, lit a cigarette and shook her head. ‘Sorry,’ she grimaced helplessly, ‘perhaps we should talk about you instead.’

‘I’m genuinely interested, really. When we took the decision to close down the magazine, we came and saw the office at the weekend. I probably saw your desk.’

‘Look, it’s really not interesting.’

‘It is, to me.’

‘All right. Mainly my job entailed a mail-sack and a pair of tongs, and the phone ringing, and messengers turning up, and the best bit was systematically throwing away all the readers’ letters to Ted’s Tips, Dear Donald and Katie’s Cuttings, because it meant Michelle had to make them all up in the evenings.’

‘You don’t like Michelle?’

‘Ha!’

‘What’s wrong with her?’

‘She’s supercilious, arch, martyrish, hostile –’

‘So you threw away the letters to Dear Donald?’

‘Yeah. Amongst other things.’ Lillian took a long drag on the cigarette and then chucked it into some dry leaves by the side of the road.

'You can start fires like that, you know.'

'Oh, give me a break.'

'Sorry.'

They walked on.

'I want to ask you something personal. When we looked around the office, I saw a corner with a lampstand and a square of carpet – was that yours?'

'Yes.' She giggled.

'Well, the funny thing is that I assumed the person who worked there must be sixty years old, at least. So I'm a bit puzzled. Here you are, talking to your husband like you're two and a half, and acting at work like you're sixty. So what I want to know is: when do you get to be your real age – when you are, if I may say so without sounding creepy and smarmy like that smarmy creep Trent Carmichael, in your prime?'

Lillian looked crestfallen.

He hesitated, but on the other hand, having got this far, he thought he'd better continue.

'I'm not a very clever man, and I don't have Margaret's knowledge, let alone her inquisitive inclinations. But on the other hand, I do wonder whether – good lord, did you see that?'

Lillian wiped a tear on her sleeve and sniffed. 'What?'

'There's someone in the garden centre.'

'Why shouldn't there be?'

'Because it's Thursday.'

'Oh.'

'Someone's broken in. And this is going to sound rather odd, but it appeared to be a chimp or a midget in a thin blue frock. You didn't see it, Lillian? On the bike?'

Lillian smiled weakly. 'I was thinking about something else.'

'You don't mind me calling you Lillian?'

'As long as you promise not to call me Bunny.'

'Fair enough.'

'So what do you want to do?'

'I'm thinking.'

But Lillian thought first.

'Didn't Tim say something about seeing Osborne abducted by a midget in a frock? I mean, it may be a *different* midget, of course, but –'

'You're right. I'd better get the others. You stay here and keep watch and I'll run back. Can you do that?'

'Of course I can.'

'Sorry, I didn't mean –' He put his hand towards her, but didn't touch. 'Right, I'll go.'

'Just one thing, though. I think Tim also mentioned a pitchfork. And it seems to me, if I rack my memory, that this may be significant, and have something to do with nipples. The figure you saw, did it have a pitchfork too?'

'I believe it did.'

'Well, in that case you'd better get your skates on.'

'Alone at last!' cackled Makepeace, flinging wide the door of the Resteezy shed, and standing arms akimbo like the jolly Green Giant. 'Ha ha ha ha ha.'

Osborne looked up wearily. He was a patient man by nature, but he was getting tired of this.

'Oh for heaven's sake, think what you're *saying*,' he said. 'We've been alone lots of times. We were alone in the van coming down here, alone in our room at Dunquenchin. We've been alone at your flat, and at mine, and in pubs and down the caff. And besides, there's the rabbit here now –'

'Stop quibbling,' said Makepeace.

'But –'

'Stop it.'

'Oh, all right.'

Makepeace struggled to recapture his former confidence. He went 'Ha ha ha, ha ha ha,' again, which helped.

'It seems to me you're not taking this seriously enough, my lily-skinned friend. Why do you think I brought you here? Why, to fulfil my fantasies with you! The whole lot. Hose, pitchfork, lawn-feed, everything – even the dibber.'

Osborne looked at him. At last he'd fallen in, after all this time. It was so simple. This man was *mad*.

'You're mad,' he said.

'I'm not.'

'You look like a chimp.'

'I don't.'

'And there's a woman behind you, about to hit you on the head with a shovel.'

'No, there isn't.'

'There is, you know,' said Lillian from behind, and with a fabulous ringing *dung*! noise, Osborne's forty-eight hours in captivity were finally brought to a close.

14

Only one thing cast a faint pall over the celebratory tea held at Dunquenchin that Thursday afternoon. Margaret Sexton had been found dead in Angela's garden.

'Grisly, really,' shuddered Trent, helping himself to another toasted teacake.

'Horrible,' agreed Michelle, spooning out some jam.

Momentarily, everyone in the room stopped laughing and chattering ('So it was you, all the time!' 'Yes, me!') and generally drawing the many laborious misunderstandings of the past few days to a satisfactory close. It was Trent who had found the body, and now all eyes turned to him, in hope of gauging his feelings. But although he made a loud burp and said, 'Excuse me,' he otherwise betrayed no sign of inner turmoil.

It looked like a suspicious death, however. Foul play was certainly indicated. Shears, rake, weed-killer, garden twine, bucket, all the usual things had been employed. Flower-pots, hose, watering-can, secateurs.

'Someone must have thought she was a real *cow*,' averred Osborne, in his innocence, and was surprised when the entire roomful of people stared guiltily into their tea.

'I suppose, to be fair, we ought to investigate,' said Gordon. 'I mean, it must have been, ahem, to coin a phrase, someone in this room that did it. In fact, pretty obviously it was Trent.'

Trent looked up, but said nothing. Gordon, embarrassed, cleared his throat and continued.

'Surely it's obvious. For a start, (a) Trent can't imagine killing anyone without popping into a garden centre first; (b) he knows most about murder; (c) he hated her; (d) she was blackmailing him; (e) she'd deceived him; and (f) he's got a new girlfriend who might have put him up to it.'

Gordon looked at the floor, his heart thumping. 'No hard feelings, of course, Mr Carmichael.'

'Of course not,' agreed Trent, with the weird smile of a man who has already killed off his young pipsqueak antagonist in his latest novel with a pair of shears. 'Goes without saying.'

Michelle loyally spooned some jam on to the back of his hand. He looked her in the eye and licked it off slowly.

'Perhaps it's not as simple as all that, anyway,' piped Angela. 'Trent doesn't know anything about real murder. And if we all start accusing each other –'

'Well, I think *you* did it!' said Michelle, jumping to her feet. 'After all, Margaret broke up your marriage!'

'She did?' shrieked Angela, jumping up likewise. 'Jesus, what a *cow*.'

Osborne felt slightly detached from all this. He didn't know Margaret. He knew Trent Carmichael only by means of his boring shed in Highgate and the lousy plots of his books. And self-evidently he could proffer no useful insight into this nasty murder, since there had been scarcely a second in the past two days when he wasn't either locked up with a long-suffering rabbit, or in bed with Angela Farmer investigating Daphne du Maurier's *Vanishing Cornwall*. So while the others debated the murder in question, he just felt sad and preoccupied. It is not every day that a friend goes bonkers and is sectioned under the Mental Health Act. When they led Makepeace to the waiting car with his arm twisted behind his blue-chiffoned back, he had uttered an extraordinary plea which would live in Osborne's memory in all his future years: 'You can't do this to me,' he said with solemnity, 'I am a contributor to *The Times Literary Supplement*.'

'I think Osborne should look into it,' said Lillian. 'He would have a fresh eye.'

'Yes, but he also doesn't know who anyone is,' snapped Trent.

'He could find out.'

'So could anybody.'

'Well, someone's got to do something.'

Angela interjected. 'Well, I think Osborne must be tired, poor baby. Don't you need a quiet lie-down?' And she waggled her eyebrows at him in a suggestive manner.

Catching the unmissable nuance of this, Michelle stifled a scream of annoyance. 'I'm phoning Mother,' she said, running from the room. 'And I think you're all mad.' She slammed the door behind her.

Angela looked around carefully. 'Hey, I think I've *been* in this play,' she said. 'And unless I'm mistaken, this is the moment when the policeman appears at the front door in a very tall helmet and we all freeze with our hands to our mouths and the curtain comes down to a cloudburst of applause.'

Things were gathering unstoppable speed. For example, when Mister Bunny stepped gingerly from the train at Honiton station, he was promptly knocked over sideways, with some violence, by a woman in a motorized wheelchair careering wildly along the platform, ostensibly out of control. It was a bad start for a visit. A litter-bin broke his fall, but possibly at the cost of a fractured rib, so the benefit was questionable. 'Aagh,' he exclaimed, clutching his dented chestal area. 'What was *that?*' His glimpsed impression was of an old, cracked-looking female in a velour track-suit shouting 'Out of my way' and 'Mind your backs' as she gouged a path through the new arrivals before hurtling towards the far end of the platform, where it ended in a sheer drop and a small pile of gravel.

'Aagh,' he repeated, staggering towards a bench and sitting down. Not only had she knocked him sideways, she'd run over his foot, leaving a nasty black mark on his Hush Puppy. In some respects, the random childlike brutality of this woman reminded him fondly of Lillian, but he cast such thoughts from his mind. After all, he was a man with a mission. Beside him he placed a small square suitcase, which he patted affectionately, evidently glad that it was safe.

'No harm done, I expect,' he said aloud, although no one was present to hear him, least of all the death-on-wheels lady, who had now mysteriously vanished.

'Oh well.' He picked up the suitcase and placed it under his arm.

'Come on,' he said, again to nobody visible. He was hobbling slightly. 'Ouch.'

Why was he here? Because, in his desperation to locate his bunnykins beloved, he had telephoned *Come Into the Garden* and spoken to Clement, the sub-editor; and against an unusually loud and echoing atmospheric clatter – suggestive of masons and electricians working inside the dome of St Paul's – Clement had explained in a raised voice about redundancy and Digger Enterprises and Honiton, and so on. Which had led Mister Bunny straight to the Honiton train.

'What's that din?' yelled Mister Bunny. 'Is somebody using an electric saw in there?'

'That's right. Well, the editor said we should take home anything we liked, and my colleague Ferdie has decided he wants to dismantle the built-in bookcases.'

'I see.'

'Which is only fair because as well as half the furniture I've got the carpets and a few of the partition walls, and the light fittings and the boiler, and the sink from the Gents.'

'What's left, then?'

Clement looked around.

'This phone. And some underlay. And the old red mark on the wall where the franking machine exploded. I was saying to Lillian, it's funny how you start off not wanting to take anything – just an angle-poise lamp or a dictionary, you know – and then somehow you can't stop, and before you know it –'

At which point, mercifully, Mister Bunny's money ran out.

'Er, do you think these tyre tracks are significant?' asked Osborne, worried that he was stating the obvious. At the scene of the crime, despite the trampling of many feet around the body (all had wanted to check that Margaret was really dead), the keen-eyed detective was able to discern a distinct and extensive criss-cross pattern of neat parallel ruts, about twenty-four inches apart. What could this mean? Osborne's brain worked rapidly. These marks were suggestive of either a motorized wheelchair doing repeated three-point-turns, or a frenzied Dalek with mud on its eyeball, or possibly a pair of novelty-act synchronized twin cyclists of outstanding technical versatility.

'Did trick cyclists kill this woman?' he said, puzzled.

Angela, Trent and Michelle gathered around to look at the evidence – the others having sensibly stayed in the warm at Dunquenchin. Osborne explained his theory, waving at the tracks in a vague but hopeful way.

'A trick cyclist homicide hit-team? That's a new one,' said Trent, fumbling in his inside pocket for a notebook and pencil.

But Michelle did not respond. She was staring at the tracks. 'I've just had a horrible thought,' she said.

Angela didn't care very much, and suggested they go inside for coffee. 'I say it was cyclists; and I say they won't get far,' she said. 'Stand out a mile in any normal setting, pirouetting on their back wheels playing Ravel's *Bolero* on the kazoo. I'd like to know their motive, that's all. What do you think, Trent? Hey, perhaps Margaret was writing a book about their unnatural love for their bikes.'

'You mean, velocipedophiles?' suggested Michelle dismally, from force of sub-editorial habit.

'Yeah. Velocipedophiles, that's *good*,' said Angela. 'Take it from me, lady, you were wasted as a nun. Velocipedophiles – you can imagine what they get up to, those sleazy bastards, greasing their pumps –'

'Riding tiny little innocent *trikes*,' added Carmichael, nodding. 'Selling illicit videos of the Tour de France –'

'But it wasn't cyclists who killed Margaret,' Michelle interrupted, with a gravity that made them both stop and listen. 'It was my mother. And I think I know why she did it.'

Angela made a tut-tut noise. 'Listen, I *have* been in this play. But for the life of me I just can't remember whether I get killed early so I can start drinking before the interval.'

Tim put down the phone and, with his eyes closed, feebly traced his way along the walls to the kitchen, where Gordon was washing up.

'That was Mrs Lewis, my next-door neighbour,' he said, stunned. 'She had a bit of bad news.'

He sat down.

'Not the cat?' Gordon sympathized.

'No, the cat's fine.'

'Oh good.'

'Yes, since the door was open, he ran out in the street. And luckily the fire engine swerved to avoid him.'

'What fire engine?'

'The one that put out the fire in my living-room.'

'Oh.'

Tim, as though in a trance, removed his spectacles and then banged his head on the kitchen table, quite hard, three times.

He put his specs back on again. 'No, it's still true,' he said. 'Oh God.'

'Was it an accident? Some thoughtless oversight?'

'No, that's the funny thing. She did it deliberately.'

'Who?'

'Mrs Lewis.'

'Why?'

'She said she was fed up with me ringing her from the office, and from here, and from tube stations, and from the corner shop, to check that the place hadn't burned down while I was away.'

'Still, it's a bit extreme.'

'That's what I said.'

'How's the damage?'

'Apparently the flat is habitable. It just looks awful and it serves me right.'

'So you can go back if you want to?'

'And she's taken the cat.'

'Oh well.'

Gordon sat down beside him, and kindly put an arm on his shoulder. Tim wanted to cry again.

'Can you show me that *Phototropism* thing you told me about? I feel I need taking out of myself.'

'All right. If you're sure. I need to tinker with it first, though, because Makepeace interfered with it somehow.'

'I can wait,' said Tim. His mind's eye was consumed with

the picture of his living-room carpet alive with flame, his Post-it notes combusting spontaneously on the door-frames like the necklace of fairy-lights around Harrods. 'Do you know what I really regret?'

'No, what?'

'That Margaret didn't live to see this moment. You see, she always upheld I was worrying about nothing.'

As Mister Bunny hobbled up the lane towards Dunquenchin, he encountered Michelle and Trent Carmichael stooped double and agitatedly tracing a set of tyre tracks in the opposite direction. 'There!' yelled Michelle. 'And there!'

'If only I had a big magnifying glass and a fancy pipe,' said Trent sarcastically.

'This isn't funny!' she snapped. 'We've got to find this wheelchair before it's too late!'

It was at the word wheelchair that Mister Bunny decided to intervene.

'Excuse me,' he said.

'Busy,' said Michelle, waving him away.

'Did you say you were looking for a woman in a wheelchair?'

'Yes, she's my mother. What's it to you?'

'Would she be wearing a track-suit?'

'Yes.'

'Then she ran over my foot at the station just five minutes ago,' said Mister Bunny, proffering his Hush Puppy for inspection. 'And I'd like to say that a more reckless –'

'The station?'

'That's right. But –'

'Trent. Come on. We've got her.'

'Perhaps you can help me, too,' Mister Bunny called after

them. 'I'm looking for a tall blonde woman in a pink coat.'

'Really?' Michelle narrowed her eyes. 'Well, be careful if you find her. I happen to know that this morning she hit a man on the head with a shovel.'

'Everything is going too fast,' said Osborne, while Angela stroked his forehead and made nice, friendly, croony noises into his ear.

'So slow down.'

'Everyone's dashing about, discovering things. We're hurtling towards the edge and there's a sheer drop and a small pile of gravel!'

'You're delirious. Perhaps it was the shock to your system of eating something other than cake.'

'I'm not used to it, that's all. I've just spent two days in cupboards.'

'So ease up.'

'It's very agitating out here. And I miss the rabbit. Is he OK?'

'He's fine. He's eating *Murder, Shear Murder*. He gave me a look that said it tasted like the gardener did it.'

Osborne rolled over. They were lying wrapped in a duvet on the sitting-room floor. Angela had pulled the curtains against the early night, switched on some lamps, and lit the fire. The only thing to ruin the mood was the music, which by an unfortunate but understandable error was not Al Bowly (as Osborne had requested) but Abba's *Greatest Hits, Volume Two*.

'Did you miss me?' shouted Osborne above the jaunty din of 'Take a Chance on Me'.

'What a question. Does cowpat stick to your shoes?'

'I missed you very much.'

'Like hell.'

'Will we keep in touch?'

'You going somewhere?'

Osborne thought about it. He pictured, for some reason, the Birthplace of Aphrodite; in particular, the woman with the grey cloth who slopped the tables while you were eating your toast, and who always put your cooked breakfast down on top of your newspaper, before you could move it out of the way.

'You don't have a job any more.'

'I know. Thanks.'

'But look on the bright side. You know a lot about celebrity sheds.'

'Oh yes. I forgot.' Osborne tried to remember when he had last seen a job advertisement that said 'Knowledge of celebrity sheds an advantage'.

'Angela, do you really think the *Observer* will snap up my column?'

'Trust me, I've got a plan. Does the name Chimneypot mean anything to you?'

'Something to do with Father Christmas?'

She tweaked his nose.

'Yeah. If you like. Something to do with Father Christmas.'

Lillian stretched out her arms, yawned and snuggled closer to the fire. Virtuous exhaustion was a novel sensation, and one to be relished. This had been a great day for her, all in all – first the searing, cleansing conversation with Gordon's dad, then the daring rescue of Osborne, followed by the modest disclaimers ('Anyone would have done the same, Michelle, but funny how it was me'), and now the peace and quiet for reflection in the cosy lounge at Dunquenchin. 'Mother Theresa of Calcutta must feel like this every day,' she thought, wiggling her toes. Somehow the mental picture of Mother Theresa panting, wiping her brow and resting on her shovel after heroically clouting a loony on the side of the head was a surprisingly pleasing one. She must mention it to Gordon's dad.

'Who was at the door?' she chirped, hearing Gordon's dad return from answering the bell. And turning, she found herself face to face with Mister Bunny.

'Bunny,' he said, simply. 'Smee.'

'Bunny. Oh.' She looked at Gordon's dad, who deliberately looked the other way.

'Er, hey-wo bunny. How doin?'

They stared at one another. Mister Bunny extended the suitcase.

'I bwung Dexie,' he explained.

'Shall I leave you?' asked Gordon's dad. 'Or shall I try to interpret?'

'No, it's all right,' said Lillian. 'Do you think we could have a cup of tea?'

'My pleasure.'

Gordon's dad paused before leaving the room, however. 'You must be Mister Bunny, then?'

Mister Bunny nodded.

'And is this Dexter, the teddy bear that's not very well at the moment?' He pointed at the tiny suitcase.

Mister Bunny nodded again.

'Well, I just can't tell you how lucky you've been in your timing. My niece Margaret would have grabbed you, chomped you and minced you up into little pieces – bones, fur, little ears, squeaker, button-eyes and all. But you will be relieved to hear she succumbed to an unexpected bombardment of garden implements today at about half-past two p.m. Cup of tea, then, Lillian?'

Mister Bunny signalled at him to wait, and then produced a cup-soup sachet from his coat pocket.

'Bunny, look, got crutongs,' he smiled.

It was a difficult moment.

'Just the tea, please, Mr Clarke,' said Lillian. And she wondered whether Mother Theresa likewise was sometimes cruel to be kind.

'Right. Hold on,' said Gordon. 'It's nearly there.'

Tim watched amazed as his new friend voyaged into the dark interior of a computer program, stooped in deep concentration over his keyboard, his body shaped like a human question mark as he tapped and thought and tapped some more. 'No wonder Makepeace went off his rocker,' Gordon commented wearily to no one in particular. And then went *tap, tap, click, tap, tap* again.

'Sorry,' said Tim, casting an eye around Gordon's office, 'but I've only just put two and two together. Did you invent *Digger*?'

'That's right.' *Tap, tap, tip, tap-tap-tap.*

'Hence Digger Enterprises?'

'Mm.' *Tap. Tip.*

'But *Digger* was enormous, Gordon. Why aren't you offensively rich?'

'I am. I just bought Frobisher's, remember.'

'But why aren't you a big company?'

'I didn't want to be.' *Tap, tap, thump.* 'I wanted to work at home. I wanted to keep my own life simple. But I've got lots of people working for me, one way or another, in the town, in London, in the US. And Dad's been marvellous.'

'Lumme. I had no idea. And this one's called *Phototropism*? I hate to be critical, Gordon, but it's not quite as catchy as *Digger*.'

'Oh, I know.' *Tap, tap, tip-tip, tap.* 'It's just provisional.'

'Would you like me to think of a name? I'm pretty good with

words, especially horticultural ones. Well, it's my job. I mean, you know. Was.'

'That would be great.' *Tap, tap, click, click, whir, tap, tap. Thump.* 'In fact, you can tell me your ideas when you get back from your journey into the unknown.'

Gordon helped him into the glove and helmet ('Sorry, specs off') and sat back.

'Just stop whenever you feel like it,' he said. 'But tell me first, what can you see?'

Tim took a while to reply.

'A really intense black,' he said at last, 'as though light has never existed.'

'Do you feel anything?'

'No. Unless, yes, the hairs of my arms are tingling. And I seem to be stretching, relaxed, turning very slowly. Am I floating?'

'Not visibly.'

'Oh, but I am. Weightless, warm, drawn out. And now there's music coming from somewhere. Gordon, you're a genius, this is beautiful.'

'What does it feel like?'

'Well. I don't know how to put this without sounding crazy, but I think I'm, um, germinating.'

'I'll shut up, then. Good luck.'

'You could call it *Come Into the Garden*. In memoriam, sort of. You could give away free packets of seeds.'

'Now you're rambling.'

'Like a wild English rose?'

'Like an idiot.'

'Bye, then.'

'See you later.'

Gordon set a stop-watch for fifteen minutes and quietly left the room. Outside, he leaned on the door.

'What's up?' said his dad, arriving with some mugs of tea. 'Gordon, you're crying.'

The boy wiped the tears from his eyes, and blew his nose in a large hanky.

'I don't know why, Dad. I just feel a lot better now, that's all.'

'How long have we known each other now?' gasped Trent Carmichael, clutching his chest as he raced to keep up with Michelle. She was steaming along the London platform at Honiton station for the third time, yelling 'Mother!'

'Since yesterday morning,' she called back.

'Is that *all*?'

They both stopped in their tracks. They could hardly believe it. Trent Carmichael leaned against a wall and wheezed.

'I don't even know, why we're doing this,' he panted. 'I've obviously lost track. You think your mother killed Margaret, using a composite of all the murder methods she'd found in my books?'

'That's right.'

'Because you had told her on the phone that you'd met the original of the girl in *S is for ... Secateurs!* which she was obsessed with?'

'That's my theory.'

'Right. Got it. So tell me this. If she's such a dangerous maniac, why on earth do we want to find her?'

'Because that's what you do to murderers. I'm surprised at you, Trent. You of all people should know that you must track them down and confront them.'

'Can we sit down?'

'What?'

'I want to sit down.'

'Why?'

'Don't look so worried, sweetheart,' he said, 'I only want to talk to you.'

With a sudden intense weariness which bleached her blood, Michelle realized what Trent Carmichael was going to say. It was brush-off time. That ghastly up-beat inflection is never used for anything else – it goes with 'It's been fun, really!' and 'I'll never forget how we found that body in the garden!' So it was all over, bar the platitudes. Here, on a cold, dark station platform, in a place she'd previously considered entirely notional ('G. Clarke, Honiton, Devon'), he would ditch her with a clear conscience and bugger off home. She tried to think positively about it, but with no job to return to, and now no mother she dare reside with, dismay promptly overwhelmed her. How predictable life is. Of course she will pretend she agrees with him ('Marvellous interlude!'), promise to come and see the famous shed ('One day!'), laugh about the hectic run of events, ask jokingly to see the novel she appears in. And then he'll get on a train and wave, and she'll know for a certainty that he's secretly thinking, 'Thank God that's over.'

'Well, Trent, it's been real,' she said bravely, trying not to cry.

'That's true,' he agreed, puzzled.

'And yes, one day I'll come and see that shed!'

'Oh. All right. Good.'

'And thanks for the autograph! I'll treasure it!' You had to hand it to her, she was taking pluck into new dimensions.

'Michelle, why are you talking like this? Are you going somewhere?'

'No. Aren't you?'

'Not unless you are. I just wanted to ask you if you fancied going back to that garden centre we passed, where Osborne was tied up. I thought you might, you know, get off on it.'

She said nothing.

'I think the pitchfork is still there,' he added.

Michelle's mouth went dry.

'Are you offended?'

'God, no.'

'So you don't mind if we give up chasing your mother?'

'Not a bit.'

'Even though I think I can hear a faint moaning coming from the end of the platform, where conceivably she tipped over the edge into a small pile of gravel?'

'Leave her.' They got up to go.

'You know something, Michelle? As a writer of crime fiction, your imagination intrigues me very deeply.'

Wincing, she put her hands to her ears.

'Just wait till I get my hands on your dangling modifiers,' she warned, saucily.

15

In the subsequent eighteen months, the following celebrity profiles and guest spots nearly (but, for reasons that will be apparent, never quite) appeared in the British press, in periodicals as divergent as *The Times*, the *Independent on Sunday*, *Radio Times*, *Old Flames* (the ex-firemen's gazette), *Which Shed? Monthly* and the *Guardian*. They are reprinted here in no particular order.

How We Met: Gordon Clarke and Timothy Johnson

The brains behind SHOOT!, the internationally bestselling ecological virtual reality program, came to partnership only last November. Clarke, 20, was the schoolboy inventor of Digger; Johnson, 24, a penniless journalist working at the sharp end of gardening tips. Famously, the name SHOOT! (a brainwave attributed to Johnson) cleverly misled thousands of adolescent boys into playing the game (or buying the home interactive video version) in expectation of violence and zap guns when in fact it soothed the savage beast and reputedly reduced violent teenage crime in Britain by a tenth in its first week of release and sale. Both men are now based part-time in Victoria, in a large empty post-modern distressed office environment – bare wires, no carpet, no sink in the Gents – and part-time in Honiton, Devon.

GORDON CLARKE: It's funny but I can't remember now what it was like not to know Tim. He's already the best friend I ever had. When we met, he had just been having some quite grisly girlfriend trouble – well, *ex*-girlfriend trouble, to be precise – and this brought us together, especially as I helped him bury the whole thing, as you might say, about six foot under. My first sight of him, I thought, 'What a weed.' It's awful but it's true. All I knew about him, before we met, was a story that in childhood he dug up some daffodil bulbs to see how they were doing. Big joke, right? But in a way, that's what I was doing both with *Digger* and *SHOOT!* – playing with the idea that dormancy is only a natural phase in the cycle of growth. So I recognized him as a kindred spirit.

Tim has an extraordinary mind, but he worries too much. If I want to know what he's thinking, I say 'What are you worrying about *now*?' and he doesn't see that there's anything odd in the question – you know, that his natural mode is worrying rather than just thinking. We suit each other because I can override a lot of this worry. He's neurotic, really. And he's obsessive. And compulsive too, I think. But the success of *SHOOT!* has helped him in lots of ways. He wears looser jumpers now. His specs don't steam up so often.

Now we are working together on a project for a new monthly gardening magazine, which he will edit. Personally, I liked the idea of calling it *Maud*, since it's the natural sequel to *Come Into the Garden*, but Tim assures me that 'Maud' is not a sexy name for a magazine. He says, imagine going into a newsagent and saying, '*Maud* out yet?' I trust Tim's judgement in these matters. He's the 'words' man, after all.

Sexually, we suit each other very well indeed. Before we met, we were both pretty hazy about our sexuality. I didn't really 'come out', as such; more sort-of turned round one day and found I was out already. My Auntie Angela says my love of musicals was an early indicator that I was gay, but I must admit I didn't suspect a thing. Tim is a lovely person. I'm going to buy him a cat for his birthday, but he doesn't know that yet.

TIMOTHY JOHNSON: I'm not sure about this. What did Gordon tell you? Are you trying to trick me into saying something that contradicts what Gordon said? Can I see a copy of what Gordon said? No, I'm sorry, I can't do it, I think we ought to stop.

On My Mantelpiece: Angela Farmer

Oh God, look, I meant to tidy it before you came but oh, what the fuck, this is meant not to be serious, right? OK, so starting from the left, a crumpled bag of peanut brittle (not mine), some shed brochures (not mine either), empty Cognac bottle (that is mine), and Trent Carmichael's new hardback, *Never the Twine Shall Meet*. (Have you read this? It's the one where an old innocent put-upon guy gets his revenge on a young psychologist by hiring a bizarre trick cyclist homicidal hit-team, and ends up living with a libidinous ex-nun he meets by chance on a train. I don't know how he thinks of them.)

What? Oh yes, mantelpiece. Then we've got a couple of scripts for new TV sitcoms (crap, actually; forget those, I'll chuck 'em out), the lease to the local garden centre (which I recently bought, when Chimneypot went bankrupt), bits of underwear, condoms. That's it. What do you mean, why do I keep condoms on the mantelpiece? To keep them away from the rabbit, why do you think?

Kitty Corner: Cat Rescue of the Month

This week we spotlight in Kitty Corner a very lucky puss rescued by Mrs Abigail Lewis, after a mysterious fire rendered him completely homeless.

'I don't know how that fire started,' says Mrs Abigail Lewis, cradling a limp, relaxed Lester in her arms like a baby, 'but I simply had to save the cat. Now he lives with me and I am making up for the neglect he suffered previously, living with the sort of person who starts fires out of sheer carelessness. Lester is a very loving cat, very sensitive. He's very fond of expensive food, unfortunately, which sometimes means I have to go without. But on the other hand, who needs adequate nutrition when they could have a wonderful little cat like Lester?

'I think he wants to have a sleep now, so perhaps you could leave. I've got his bed made up with a hot-water bottle and a fleecy blanket, and I've drawn the curtains just the way he likes them. So I just have to kiss each of his paws – mwah! mwah! mwah! mwah! – and tickle his ears, and rest his catnip toy on his white linen pillow, and tiptoe out again. Bless him. Oh yes, sometimes I lie on the floor next to him, in case he wakes up and wants something.'

My TV Dinner: Angela Farmer

It depends who's cooking, you see. If it's me we might just have a big drink, a piece of cheese and a slice of fruitcake, but if my lover-baby is cooking (if that's the right word – I mean 'cooking', not 'lover-baby') he's a lot more inventive, especially with tinned stuff, which he mixes together, cold. No, it's fine. Really. Don't worry about me, I can take it.

And it's a real scream to watch, too. A subtle transformation occurs as he stirs it all together in a big bowl with a trowel. Tuna, baked beans, sweetcorn, rice pudding, peach slices. I've learned a lot. It's amazing how many different ways food can resemble puke.

A Life in the Day: Trent Carmichael

I rise at nine on most days, listen to the radio for its edifying effect on my imagination, and depending on how exhausted I am from yesterday's efforts (at writing, I mean) return to bed with a cup of delicately fragranced herb tea for another snooze. Writing is very hard work, people should realize, especially when one is forever inventing very complicated murder plots involving Spear & Jackson garden implements in new and breathtaking combinations! People tell me I've made a rod for my own back with all these secateurs and buckets, but I don't see it that way, it's what I'm famous for, and I'm grateful. I mean, did Will Shakespeare ever complain, 'They keep demanding the same old blank verse, but I am an artist, I want to express myself in limerick and knock-knock jokes'? Personally, I ain't convinced.

My girlfriend, Michelle, is a great help to me, she's one in a million, especially when she changes all my prose and rescues me from silly grammatical mistakes. She's a whizz on my computer, evidently, although actually I've never shown her how to use it. In fact, quite the contrary – I keep changing the password. But even when I finish the day by putting my latest writing in a secret file, she still manages to find it! I might pop down to the shops for a new box of paper and when I get back and switch on the machine, my stuff has been rigorously rewritten, and the original discarded. What an amazing woman. Even when I write in longhand, and hide the sheets of paper in the shed in a special hole under the floorboards, I still find – when I retrieve it – that it's covered in bright blue sub-editing marks, with comments such as 'Cliché?' added in the margins. I don't know what I'd do without her. I'm thinking of including her in the next book, but I haven't thought how to 'do' her yet, if you catch my drift.

In the afternoons I sometimes go for walks, and think about my characters as though they were real people. Actually, this isn't as clever as it sounds, since most of them *are* real people. But when I need a new twist in the plot, I like to go off by myself and stand on the horizon at Parliament Hill with my head thrown back in a thoughtful pose. You could take my picture doing that, if you like. The twin cyclists in my new book, for example, I know what you're thinking, 'Where on earth would an idea like that come from?' Well, it was simply divine inspiration. All I can tell you is that I just *needed* those trick cyclists, and suddenly, with a sweet *tring! tring!* of bicycle bells, there they were.

I quite often do readings in bookshops in the evenings. As you know, my books are extremely popular, so it's a surprise when so few people turn up. But my publisher assures me that many of my most devoted fans are simply infirm – in wheelchairs, nursing homes, hospitals for the criminally insane – and can't get down to the bookshops for the readings. Which sounds plausible. We sometimes laugh about it. I mean, as long as it doesn't prevent them from buying the books, they can be as sick as they like, I don't care.

Dinner is usually at home. Just Michelle and me, or should that be 'Michelle and I'? – either way, just the two of us. It's lucky we enjoy one another's company, because curiously we don't have any friends. Michelle tried to make some once, in the West Country, but with predictably hilarious results (as they say in the *Radio Times!*). So we spend our evenings plotting murders and testing out certain new plot devices in the seclusion of our own home, behind drawn curtains, not hurting anybody, and sometimes recording it on video. Michelle is usually as ready as I am for a bit of excitement when evening comes, as she spends a lot of her day in the unrewarding job of returning letters to fans with all their mistakes helpfully crossed out and altered.

And so to bed. When I lie awake at night I sometimes think up names for new books, as it helps me get to sleep. My good friend Angela Farmer sometimes jokes that it takes me less time to write my books than to think of the titles, which I think, in common with all jokes, has a tiny element of truth in it! But now I have Michelle to help, and she is very good at it, so I've already got a stockpile of fifteen decent titles to be going on with. The next six months are going to be tough!

Where Did You Get That? – Angela Farmer

Where did I get *what*? Don't you people have anything better to do? Oh for the love of Mike. I've got to go now, I've got my leg caught in a man-trap.

Dagenham Delights

This week local woman Mrs Lillian Bugs tells us how she and her husband changed their name by deed poll to something less silly, under advice from a Harley Street psychotherapist specializing in regression in couples.

'We're much better now,' says ex-Mister Bunny', in all seriousness, while waggling his ears and doing the goofy thing with his teeth.

My Perfect Weekend – Angela Farmer

Where would you go? Somewhere where nobody asked me celebrity questions all the time.

How would you get there? By a miracle.
Where would you stay? In bed.
Who would be your perfect companion? My rabbit. I mean, no, my local shed-dealer. It's a long story.
What essential piece of clothing would you take? Bandanna.
Which books would you read? '101 Uses of a Bandanna'.
What three things would you most like to do? Have a quiet time with the rabbit. Have a quiet time with my shed-dealer. Have a quiet time with my bandanna.
What would you like to find when you got home? That I was the only kid on my block who knew enough about bandannas to improvise a makeshift bunny-hammock for a tired rabbit.

Old Flame of the Month: Henry Clarke

Ten years after Henry Clarke left the fire service, he is now embarking on a whole new life, and asks his old cronies to 'Come on Down!' to a new garden centre in Honiton, where he is in charge of water gardens, ponds and fountains. 'Can't seem to stay away from water!' he jokes.

'But there is a lot more besides at the new Angela Farmer Garden Centre (formerly known as Chimneypot). Visit our amazing shed museum, in which sheds of the famous have been painstakingly reconstructed, using genuine tools, bags of manure, cat-litter, Christmas decorations and carrier-bags full of carpet off-cuts, to represent – in exact replica! – sheds belonging to Harold Wilson, Zsa Zsa Gabor, Jane Seymour and Frank Bough. The idea came from Osborne Lonsdale, who also gives a free guided tour of the exhibit, with anecdotes! No, it's very interesting. Where are you going? Oh, give us a break.'

What I'm Reading – Angela Farmer

I can't believe you guys, you never give up. Every time I answer the phone! Well, what I like best are self-help books because they're hilarious. I'm reading one about improving your telephone technique at the moment, you know, concentration, courtesy, staying awake, not rambling, that sort of thing. Hang on, sorry – *You! Rabbit! Stop eating those condoms immediately!* Get *down*, for Pete's sake! Sorry, what was I saying, I've forgotten. Oh yes, self-help books. And there's another one I've got which helps you remember where you've seen someone before, and I find that very interesting because there's someone I can't place – all day I'm saying, 'Where, oh where, oh where did I meet him?' You know? – and it's bugging me.

Hang on, sorry – *I told you before! Do that again and, cute as you are, you'll end up as PIE! Got that?* Sorry, just talking to the boyfriend, he's making disgusting food again, and I just won't stand for it any longer. Yeah, anyway, this book tells you to look at the mystery person kinda sideways, so I keep doing that, but all it does is make him nervous.

How We Met: Angela Farmer and Osborne Lonsdale

ANGELA FARMER: For God's sake, I keep explaining, we *can't remember*. Osborne thinks it might be something to do with the theatre, because he used to review plays in the sixties and early seventies, but I'm not so sure.

OSBORNE LONSDALE (quietly): She keeps squinting at me. It's scary.

FARMER: The trouble is, it's not bugging him, it's only bugging me. He says we'll probably just remember one day –

LONSDALE: One day, yes –

FARMER: But meanwhile I've gone nutsy cuckoo, you see, so that's why I asked you to see us together, because it might concentrate his mind a bit and get the whole thing sorted out.
LONSDALE: Or it might not.
FARMER: Thanks. So, Mister 'Independent on Sunday', perhaps you could ask us some questions, to get the ball rolling?
INTERVIEWER (hesitantly): Um, OK. Er, you might not believe this but actually I'm a clairvoyant with exceptional powers, and I can probably *tell* you how you met, if you really want to know.
FARMER: What? Really? (To Lonsdale) Can you believe this?
LONSDALE: No.
FARMER (to interviewer): Sir, have you ever heard the theatrical expression *deus ex machina?*
INTERVIEWER: I don't think so.
FARMER: Well, that's a relief, because I don't know what it means. OK, so tell us, how did we meet, then? Do you need any special records on, and the curtains closed, and that kind of thing?
INTERVIEWER: No, but it would be nice to hold the rabbit.
FARMER: OK. I don't imagine you're going to print this, are you?
INTERVIEWER: I doubt it.
FARMER: Then I'd just like to say this is the best interview, aside from Osborne's, I've ever had.
INTERVIEWER: Thanks. I'm drifting off, now. Would you like to hold hands? It doesn't add anything from my point of view, but you do seem very fond of each other. Anyway, I see a garden shed. I hear muffled screams –
LONSDALE (gasps): Not Makepeace?

INTERVIEWER: I see a figure in a gypsy cloak unlocking the door. There is a name beginning with 'B'.

FARMER (with a shriek): It's Barney's. I let you out of Barney's shed!

LONSDALE: Did you?

FARMER: That's it! A kid had locked you in!

LONSDALE: Oh, good. Right. Lovely. So that's solved that, then. You can stop giving me those funny looks.

INTERVIEWER (still in trance): It's a 'B', but I can't quite get the rest. Is it Benny? Bradley?

FARMER: I just told you, it's Barney.

INTERVIEWER (unhearing, in a world of his own): Possibly Bailey, but I'm sticking my neck out.

FARMER (ignoring him): Well, so: Barney's shed. Phew, that's a weight off my mind.

LONSDALE: But I don't understand what you were doing at Barney's house when the kid locked me in the shed. Wasn't it ages after the divorce?

FARMER: Well, I was upset. And like any spurned first wife, naturally I was hanging around his new home and hoping to scatter bits of glass in the kiddies' sand-pit under the guise of an old, gnarled gypsy woman selling hub-caps door to door.

LONSDALE: Hub-caps?

FARMER: Something, yeah. Actually I think it *was* hub-caps. But he saw through my disguise.

INTERVIEWER (to himself): Brierley, was it? Baloney?

LONSDALE: What do we do about the chap in the trance?

FARMER: He didn't say anything about waking him up, did he?

LONSDALE: Better leave him, you think?

INTERVIEWER: Battersby? Bombay?

FARMER: Sure. He looks quite happy, with the rabbit.

INTERVIEWER: Bali Hai? Broccoli? Bambi?

My Childhood: Trent Carmichael

My childhood was absolutely normal in every respect, and nothing horrible ever happened to me to make me become a crime novelist, if that's what you're angling after. I had a mother and father who loved me enough to call me Trent and give me a start in life. I did all the usual childish proto-writer things, such as reading indoors when everyone else was playing rough games, and learning poetry by rote so as to be teacher's pet. That's not too revealing, is it? I mean, that's normal. We had holidays in Sussex, and I enjoyed Knickerbocker Glories, but I don't think it warped me in any way at all. You can't read anything into a Knickerbocker Glory. Thank you, I really enjoyed doing that. Smashing.

The Questionnaire: Angela Farmer

What is your idea of perfect happiness? Someone to love me, and not run out.

What is your greatest fear? That he'll run out.

With which historical figure do you most identify? Cinderella, maybe. Snow White. All those pathetic innocents. Sleeping Beauty.

Which living person do you most admire? The confident woman who lives inside my answering machine and who tells me the time the messages arrived. She harbours not a single doubt in the whole fibre of her being.

What is the trait you most deplore in yourself? My inability to refuse interviews.

What is the trait you most deplore in others? Their need to ask questions.

What vehicles do you own? Why? Are you an out-of-work mechanic, or something? Who the hell wants to know what vehicles I own? I have a *car*.

What is your greatest extravagance? Long-distance phone

calls to London newspapers, to apologize for being snappy.

What objects do you always carry with you? Castrol GTX, bit of rag, spanners, overalls, tyre levers, jump leads, battery recharger, spare wiper blades.

What makes you most depressed? Running out of drink before 7 p.m. on a Sunday.

What do you most dislike about your appearance? That I've got crow's-feet. But on the other hand, it's worse for the crow that's got mine.

What is your most unappealing habit? I dig stuff out of my ears and then eat it.

Which words or phrases do you most overuse? 'Ech! Earwax!'

What or who is (was) the greatest love of your life? My last ex-husband, see below.

Which living person do you most despise? My last ex-husband, see above.

What is your favourite smell? The Tahitian gardenia on the tropical hillside of Hana Iti in French Polynesia. Sorry, that's not true. Um, gin and tonic.

What is your favourite word? Glenmorangie.

What is your favourite building? How many buildings do you think I've got?

What is your favourite journey? Back from the off-licence.

What do you consider the most overrated virtue? Abstemiousness.

On what occasions do you lie? Whenever I find sitting too strenuous.

What is your greatest regret? That I am too good at acting to appear in *The House of Eliott*.

When and where were you happiest? When Osborne, my new chap, said he would stay in Honiton if there was a reasonably good peanut-brittle supplier, and we found out there was.

How do you relax? By pottering in the garden. I also do diggering, prunering and weedering.
What single thing would improve the quality of your life? Less work.
Which talent would you most like to have? To do less work, and not worry about it.
What would your motto be? Something will turn up.
What keeps you awake at night? Nothing. Not even sheds burning down.
How would you like to die? Is that a threat?
How would you like to be remembered? That's very kind of you. Yes, I'd like that a lot.

Quote of the Month (Sheds) – Osborne Lonsdale

'I don't know how I got into sheds, but the funny thing is this. Once you're in them, it's very hard to get out again.'

GOING LOCO
Lynne Truss

If there were more than one of you, could you run your life more easily? Belinda Johansson is a freelance critic and novelist trying to have it all and not really coping.

Her house and domestic affairs are in chaos; if only she had a double, she would get so much more done. Deep in research for her *magnum opus* – a definitive account of the *doppelgänger* in classic gothic fiction – she fails to notice the echoes of these ghoulish tales disturbingly close at hand. For not only is the cleaning lady taking over her life, but the identity of her husband, Stefan, is in question. Is he a harmless geneticist from Sweden, or actually a cunning clone? Why is the cleaning lady's previous employer having a breakdown, and what on earth has a rat circus got to do with any of this?

Going Loco is a kaleidoscope in which identities shift with alarming ease, a cautionary tale for dizzying times and, quite simply, the funniest novel you could only ever hope to read about outlandish fish cookery, men in skirts and ... Abba.

'Lynne Truss lets her imagination explode in what can only be described as a riddle devised while coming down off hallucinogens ... The book sings with glittering prose' – *Time Out*

ISBN 1 86197 733 6

MAKING THE CAT LAUGH
Lynne Truss

For eighteen long years Lynne Truss has tried to make her cat laugh. It has been an uphill task, and this book is recognition of outstanding courage in the face of futility. The cat remains unimpressed.

Never have so many jokes about Kitbits been found in such concentration as in *Making the Cat Laugh*. However, under headings such as 'The Single Woman Considers Going Out but Doesn't Fancy the Hassle' and 'The Single Woman Stays at Home and Goes Quietly Mad', we discover a writer not only obsessed with her cats, but prone to over-reacting generally to news stories ('Dead Man "Eaten" in Gruesome Cat Horror'), shopping, passive smoking ,Christmas, coupledom, boyfriends, snails, sheds, Andre Agassi, cooking instructions, requests of 'How's the novel going?' and personal remarks of any kind.

'A small masterpiece of comedy ... with abundant close observation, the familiar is made fresh ... A continual hoot' – *The Times*

ISBN 1 86197 754 9

TENNYSON'S GIFT
Lynne Truss

It is July 1864 and the Isle of Wight is buzzing with eccentric creative types. Tennyson recites poetry to furniture while his invalid wife hides bad reviews in teapots and buries them in the garden with a teaspoon. Also at Freshwater Bay are the creepy Charles Dodgson (aka Lewis Carroll) and Julia Margaret Cameron, a photographer determined to capture an image of the bard in a suitably heroic pose. Into this cauldron of unrequited love and egotism step the acclaimed painter G. F. Watts and his unlikely 16-year-old actress wife Ellen Terry; also the American father-and-daughter team of phrenologists, Lorenzo and Jessie Fowler.

A Carrollian comic novel about mid-Victorian highbrows? About the ideals of Beauty, Art, Friendship, Gratitude and Serious Beards? The only wonder is that nobody thought of it before. Unexpectedly moving and luminously wise, *Tennyson's Gift* is the funniest novel ever written about a nineteenth-century Poet Laureate.

'The perfect summer book. No deck-chair will be complete without it.' – *Independent*

ISBN 1 86197 713 1